Weekly Reader Children's
Book Club presents

The Treasure
of Kilvarra

The Treasure of Kilvarra

by Elizabeth Baldwin Hazelton

Illustrations by Marilyn Miller

Xerox Family Education Services

XEROX

Publishing, Executive, and Editorial Offices:
Xerox Family Education Services
Middletown, Connecticut 06457

ISBN 0-88375-204-2
Library of Congress Catalogue Card Number: 74–75200

For Jane and Steve,
in celebration of all the years remembered
and the years to be

Contents

*The Treasure
of Kilvarra*

1

An Irish Surprise

Christie MacAlistaire's blue eyes were shining with delight. "Just think," she said, "I'm eleven years old today, and we're in Ireland!"

"And yesterday you were only ten and we were home in Oregon, six thousand miles away," said her brother, Kevin, who was thirteen.

"It's almost too exciting to believe," said Christie.

"I believe it," said Kevin, "with Mom driving a foreign car on the wrong side of the road."

"Wrong in Oregon, right in Ireland," said his mother, "and you'd better help me to remember which is which."

She was piloting the unfamiliar Hillman down the single street of a small Irish town where the houses and shops stood wall-to-wall, fronting onto the narrow sidewalk.

"Look out, Mom! They're both wrong!" said Kevin suddenly, as they rounded a bend in the road.

"Sheep—and little lambs!" Christie gasped ecstatically, as her mother braked to a stop.

"Wow!" said Kevin. "It's a whole flock and they're coming right at us. What do we do now?"

"We sit tight," said his mother, letting the motor idle.

The sheep, looking round and bulgy with their thick dust-stained wool, filled the street from one side to another, so that no car could pass in either direction. Behind the sheep, a man riding a bicycle urged them forward.

Leading the flock, six little lambs were running beside their mothers. Their short thick wool was new and white, but their tiny knees were black from kneeling in the moist earth of the meadows. As the sheep behind them pushed them forward toward the car, the lambs began to jump around nervously, making shrill little cries of "mah-m-m-m, mah-m-m-m, mah-m-m-m" and crowding closer to their mothers.

"They're frightened," said Christie in distress, as Mrs. MacAlistaire shut off the motor.

"And dumb," said Kevin. "I hope they have the sense to go around us."

"They're not dumb, they're just babies," said Christie defensively, and rolling down the car window, she knelt on the seat and leaned out toward them. Her blonde hair fell forward around her face and she brushed it back with one hand, while she reached out with the other and made tender crooning sounds to reassure them.

Perhaps they sensed the love in her voice, or perhaps the nearness of a human being took their attention away from the automobile, for they stopped jumping and scampered safely around it.

"I touched one!" said Christie, her voice hushed with wonder. "It was so soft! Oh Mommy, six lambs! I never saw anything so adorable."

The sheep went by quickly and the shepherd, tipping his cap and smiling, rode after his flock.

Mrs. MacAlistaire started the motor. "Now do you believe you're in Ireland?" she asked.

"I'll say I do!" said Christie blissfully.

"I'd rather see horses," Kevin said. "I wonder if Mr. O'Flaherty has any Connemara ponies."

"We'll soon find out," his mother said.

They had passed the small cluster of buildings that made up the town, and now the road stretched ahead through green pastureland sprinkled with yellow and white daisies. Wind-blown clouds darkened the color of one field while the sun brightened another, and the walls of gray stone that divided them made the whole countryside look like a patchwork quilt.

"D'you mean one of these farms could be Mr. O'Flaherty's?" Kevin asked, his brown eyes sparkling with excitement.

"I think it's time to begin watching," his mother said.

Kevin and Christie examined the landscape eagerly. Scattered here and there, small farmhouses with whitewashed walls and slate roofs stood in the midst of their fields, some of them with doors and window frames painted in bright red or lime green or yellow. Each house had its own stone sheds and barns nearby, and a few looked like remnants of old ruins, as if in this place centuries ago someone's house—perhaps even a castle—had been destroyed, leaving only a small part of it standing for the present owners to reclaim.

"It isn't one of these," Christie said positively. "It has an old-fashioned thatched roof."

"Who told you that?" Kevin asked.

"*Our* Mr. O'Flaherty, of course," said Christie.

"Our" Mr. O'Flaherty was Terence O'Flaherty, the owner of the general store in the town on the Oregon coast where they'd spent their vacation last summer. The first day they'd gone into his store he had shown them his trick of blowing the smoke from his calabash pipe out of his ears, and they had become friends.

Their friend, Terence O'Flaherty, had been born in the very farmhouse for which they were looking, but the Mr. O'Flaherty who lived there now with his elderly mother was Padraic, his brother.

Terence O'Flaherty had been elated when he'd heard that Kevin's and Christie's father was going to Ireland for conferences with a famous professor of music and taking his family with him. He had insisted that they must go to visit his mother and Padraic and see what it was like to live on a farm in the west of Ireland.

Their father had left them at Shannon International Airport and flown on to Dublin for his meeting with the professor at Trinity College. They would join him there later.

But the prospect of seeing the famous city of Dublin was not nearly as exciting to Kevin and Christie as the thought of the Irish farm. And more than that, the two surprises that awaited them there. For that was what Terence O'Flaherty had promised them: two surprises, one entirely different from the other.

"You know about the surprises, Mom," Kevin

said. "Now that we're almost there, can't you give us a hint?"

"Now that you're almost there you don't need a hint," said Mrs. MacAlistaire mischievously.

She continued to drive to the northwest, with Kevin and Christie scanning the farmhouses along the way and searching for the name of O'FLAHERTY which Padraic was to put out on a road post to guide them.

"Wait, Mommy—stop a minute!" Christie burst out suddenly. "There's a lovely pond with swans!"

Mrs. MacAlistaire checked the rear view mirror and braked the car to a stop. Across the road, a grassy bank scattered with daisies sloped down gently to meet the water. Tall reeds stood high along the fringes of the pond, and long green grasses with white blossoms floated on the surface. Two swans sailed regally along the far shore, and on the embankment above them stood a farmhouse with a hill behind it, covered with trees.

"It's got a thatched roof," said Kevin. "Maybe this is the O'Flaherty place."

"Oh, I hope so!" said Christie fervently. "It's the most beautiful farm I've ever seen."

Mrs. MacAlistaire drove forward slowly while they searched for the signpost. The sun was dipping toward the horizon, turning the water of the pond to a shimmering gold.

"I see the sign," Kevin shouted. "Pull up, Mom—this is it!"

His mother turned off the highway onto a dirt road that curved around the end of the pond and wound upslope toward the house.

At that moment, Kevin spotted something in the

pasture that stretched away to their left. "Wow!" he exclaimed in amazement. "What's that?"

Christie and her mother followed his gaze and saw a strange sort of encampment at the opposite end of the field. There were covered wagons and a big tent and two-wheeled carts, all placed in a circle around a campfire, with people tending it and children playing.

"It's a Gypsy caravan," said Mrs. MacAlistaire.

"Gypsies!" Kevin was astonished.

"Irish Gypsies. They're also called 'tinkers' and sometimes 'travelers,'" his mother explained, "because they roam all over the country in their wagons and carts. They've camped here every spring since Terence O'Flaherty was a boy."

Christie was entranced. "I'll bet they're one of our surprises!" she exclaimed.

"Surprise number one," her mother admitted, "and we're very lucky to arrive when they're here, for they stay only a short time."

"They've got horses!" Kevin burst out exuberantly. "Real beauties, grazing out there beyond the wagons."

"I wonder if the Gypsies tell fortunes," said Christie.

"Maybe—" her mother said.

Christie's eyes glistened with anticipation. "Wouldn't it be fabulous to have my fortune told by a real Gypsy on my birthday!"

"I wouldn't want mine told," said Kevin candidly. "If they're fakes it doesn't mean anything, and if they're good, they might tell you something you wouldn't want to hear."

But Christie was not to be deterred. "I'd take a chance," she said.

They had stopped to look at the Gypsies, and now they saw a man coming down the road toward them. They knew at once that he was Padraic O'Flaherty. He was a bit taller than Terence, and his farmer's body was lean and hard under his flannel shirt and tweed trousers. His hair was white and thick, and his face was surprisingly young, with fair clean-shaven skin, but he had the same strong features and the same twinkling blue eyes as his brother.

They got out of the car, and he hurried to meet them with a welcome so warm they felt as if they were already friends.

"I see that you have discovered the tinkers," he said, with a knowing look at Mrs. MacAlistaire.

"Could we go over to see them now, sir, before it gets dark?" asked Kevin, unable to contain his excitement.

His mother started to protest, but Padraic said, "Indeed we can, and a good time it is for going. My mother is baking a pot oven cake for tea, and it's not yet ready." He glanced toward the farmhouse above the pond. "She's up there now, watching us," he said.

In the open doorway, they could see the slight figure of a woman in a dark dress with a white apron and shawl. They waved to her and she waved back.

"You run along with Mr. O'Flaherty, then, and I'll go up and help his mother with tea," said Mrs. MacAlistaire, sliding in behind the steering wheel.

"There's no need—" Padraic began.

"But I'd like to," she said with a smile. "I can see

the Gypsies later."

The sun was sinking into an Irish mist as she drove up toward the house, and the wind blowing in from the Atlantic had an icy chill. Kevin and Christie were glad of the heavy hand-knit sweaters their mother had bought them at Shannon Airport. Christie put on the warm woollen beret that matched hers, but Kevin let his thick shock of brown hair blow in the breeze as they started across the field with Mr. O'Flaherty.

"Sir, could you tell us why the Gypsies are called 'tinkers'?" Kevin asked.

"I could and I will," said Padraic, as they followed the track of the wagons. "It's because they used to be tinsmiths, and they traveled the road, stopping to work wherever there were pots and pans to be mended. But nowadays it's cheaper to buy new ones in the shops, so there's no tinwork to be done anymore."

"Then what work do they do?"

"Some do little work at all," said Padraic, with a smile. Kevin and Christie guessed that there was more to be told than he was telling. "But some of the men are good at catching wild horses and taming them, and then they sell or trade them at fairs."

"Did they tame the ones they've got here?" Kevin asked.

"They did," said Padraic, "and fine Connemara ponies they are, but too wild for any but the Gypsies to tame."

"Golly!" breathed Kevin, awed at the thought.

They were nearer to the camp now, and though the mist was hastening the darkness, they could see the caravan much more clearly. The wagons were painted a rich maroon color, with the spikes of the wheels a bright yellow, and the rounded hoods a blue-green, and each had a small chimney sticking up out of the top. Between them was a grayish-black tent large enough to sleep several people, but in addition there were beds of straw on the two-wheeled pony carts, protected by small canvas tops.

The fire in the center of the circle was roaring now, and the Gypsies were clustered around it as the cold of the night began to come down upon them. A black-bearded man of about Padraic's age was playing a fiddle, and a younger man was accompanying him with a wheezing accordion. They could hear the music mixed with the soft whisper of the wind. Kevin and Christie could hardly believe it was real.

"Do they tell fortunes?" Christie asked in a hushed voice.

"They do indeed," said Padraic. "Would you be wanting your fortune told?"

"Oh, yes!" Christie whispered eagerly.

"Are they any good?" Kevin cut in.

"Good!" Padraic hooted softly. "There's no one better in the whole of Ireland than the old woman, Sorcha O'Halloran. Descendant of an Irish chieftain of the north, she is. Executed more than three hundred years ago, he was, for saving the lives of shipwrecked sailors of the Spanish Armada, in the wars with the English. Her people were dispossessed of their lands because of it, and brought down to starvation in the time of the great famine. That's when they became Gypsies."

Kevin was speechless with surprise.

"There were Romany Gypsies here in the days when Sorcha was a young girl," Padraic went on.

"Wanderers from the ends of the earth, they were, and one of them— an old woman, it was—discovered that Sorcha had the gift of seeing into the future. It was then she taught her all their secret wisdom."

"Wow!" said Kevin. "She's *too* good. You'd better skip it, Chris."

"No," Christie protested, "I want to know what's going to happen to us, here in Ireland. It's such a special place."

"It is indeed," Padraic agreed. "There's no other like it in the world, and that's the truth."

"There, you see!" said Christie conclusively. "It could be something very exciting, and if it happens to me it will happen to you too, Kevin, because we're together."

"Not necessarily," said Kevin, "and in this place, it could be something scary. Don't forget that!"

"Whichever it is," said Padraic, "the question is, can we get old Sorcha to tell us?"

"But you said they told fortunes," Christie reminded him.

"That they do. The old woman has taught her daughter-in-law, Kate, to read the cards, but it is Sorcha you'll be wanting."

"Oh, yes!" said Christie.

"But we can't count on it," said Padraic. "It's tired she is, with ninety years of roaming in her old body, and she does little now but rock in her chair by the fire and sleep."

"Can't we ask her?" Christie pleaded.

"We can," said Padraic, "but she will not do it unless she chooses. I'll take you to her, and she will look into your eyes and decide."

2

The Gypsy's Prophecy

As they approached the Gypsies, both Christie and
Kevin singled out the figure of the old woman immediately. She was seated in a battered old rocker
near the warmth of the fire, and she had drawn her
hooded black cloak so closely around her that it was
impossible to tell whether she was awake or asleep.

In her heart, Christie was praying that she was
awake, for she was sure that no one would want to
disturb her slumber, and now more than ever she
wanted to hear what the remarkable Sorcha might
tell her.

They came first to the black-bearded fiddler, who
stopped playing and rose from his blanket on the
ground to greet Padraic and to meet Christie and
Kevin. He was old Sorcha's son, Seamus O'Halloran,
and his fiddle had been made by his grandfather
more than one hundred years ago. The handsome
red-cheeked woman beside him was his wife, Kate,

and Christie realized that she would be the one to tell her fortune if the old woman were asleep.

But at that moment, a drowsy voice came out of the shadows under the black hood. "Seamus," it complained, "why is it you have stopped the music?"

Old Sorcha had stirred only because she had missed the lilting Irish waltz. She didn't know that Padraic had come to the camp bringing guests—or perhaps she was just pretending not to know. If that were true, Christie thought, then she would be in no mood to read the cards.

"Play, Seamus, Bartley, play now again!" she commanded, her voice deeper and stronger, though her face was still hidden by the hood.

"Yes, Mother, we will indeed," Seamus said soothingly, and he picked up the melody where he had left off.

The tall dark man with the accordion began to accompany him softly, while Padraic introduced him. He was Bartley O'Halloran, the son of Seamus, and grandson of Sorcha.

Hearing the waltz, the old woman sighed deeply, as if she were drifting off contentedly to sleep, and Christie feared that her chances were drifting with her.

Padraic was introducing them to Bartley's wife and children now, and Christie saw only that the woman was very pretty, with red hair and green eyes, and that there were five children. Their names seemed to float around her in the air—Bridgie and Shawn, Neddie and Mick and Jill—but she couldn't keep them sorted out because her mind was full of the old woman. She wondered how she could make

the old Gypsy look into her eyes and decide in her
favor.

Then she realized that Padraic was calling to a
boy she hadn't seen before. He was coming down
the steps of one of the caravan wagons, a lean bare-
foot boy with red curly hair and freckles, and on top
of his head stood a crow.

Kevin was staring at him just as she was, hardly
believing what he saw.

Padraic was saying, "This is Colum O'Halloran,
great grandson of Sorcha, and about your age,
Kevin. It's fourteen you are now, isn't it, Colum?"

"It is," said Colum soberly.

"I'm going on fourteen," said Kevin. Then he
grinned. "But I
won't get there for
almost eight months."

Colum didn't smile,
but continued to
regard them solemnly,
and they noticed that
he had green eyes
flecked with gold.
But it was hard for
them to look at him
closely with the crow
on his head.

"His name is Ben,"
Colum volunteered.

Surprisingly, Ben
said a low word in
his throat.

"Does he talk?"

asked Kevin.

"To be sure!" said Colum gravely. "But you wouldn't understand him."

"Why not?" Christie asked.

"He speaks in Gaelic," said Colum.

"What's that?" Kevin asked.

"That's the ancient tongue of the Irish," said Padraic O'Flaherty. "It is much spoken here in the west—"

Ben interrupted loudly with what sounded like a whole sentence.

"Was that Gaelic?" asked Christie in astonishment.

"It was," Colum declared, "and I can tell you what he said."

"What?" asked Kevin suspiciously.

"He said, 'It's getting dark and time for me to go to roost.'"

To their amazement, Ben gurgled another word or two that might as well have been "You're right!" and flew back to his perch above the door of the caravan wagon, just under the shelter of the hood.

"Ha! What did I tell you?" Colum bragged. He didn't crack a smile, but he couldn't quite hide the glint of mischief in his odd green-gold eyes.

The crow croaked once more and then settled in on his roost.

"I suppose that time he said 'Goodnight,' " said Kevin, catching on.

Colum grinned. "That he did."

"Did you tame him?" Kevin asked.

"I did," Colum said. "He fell out of a nest in the

rookery when his mouth was bigger than his tail. I found him and raised him up. He was so small I named him Ben Bola for the giant that sleeps under the mountains in Connemara."

The mention of Connemara reminded Kevin of the ponies, but the dusk was deepening into darkness and he knew it was too late to see them now.

"Can you tame horses?" he asked.

"I can!" Colum boasted.

"Will you teach me?"

Colum shook his head. "No, that I cannot," he said importantly. "The way of the taming is a Gypsy secret."

"But you will take Kevin to see the horses in the morning," said Padraic.

"That I will, sir," Colum promised.

Christie's thoughts had turned back to Sorcha O'Halloran. The old woman was still huddled into the folds of her cloak, but now she was rocking gently, as if she were keeping time to the music.

"I think she's awake!" Christie whispered to Padraic.

Padraic saw the rocking and nodded. "Come," he said quietly, "I will take you to her, but we will not speak of the fortune at first. We will wait."

He took Christie's hand and led her around the circle until they were directly in front of the old woman.

"Sorcha!" he called softly.

There was no response. Old Sorcha continued to rock and her face, deep in the shadow of her black hood, was invisible. The two men with fiddle and accordion went on playing, though their music was more subdued, and the members of the Gypsy family watched but no one spoke.

"Sorcha!" Padraic called, a little louder this time. "It's Padraic."

The rocking stopped. "Padraic, is it?" The voice sounded surprised, and Christie realized that old Sorcha must have been listening to the music with her eyes closed and had not heard Padraic the first time. Now she leaned forward, peering out of the threadbare black hood, and the glow of the fire lighted her face.

It was a very old face, thin and wrinkled, but the mark of her aristocratic ancestors lingered in the high cheek bones and the dark, deep-set eyes, sunken but proud.

"It's a friend from America I have brought to see you," Padraic was saying. "Christie MacAlistaire, she is, who has come with her mother and her brother, Kevin, to visit me."

Christie wanted to speak, but her voice failed her and she stood stunned into silence by the penetrating look of the old woman's eyes. Sorcha did not speak either, but continued to stare at her as if she were seeing right through her.

Was this the look Padraic had been talking about? Christie wondered. No, it couldn't be. Sorcha couldn't be deciding about telling her fortune, because she hadn't even asked her yet. Unless, Christie thought, she was seeing the question in her mind.

She knew she should be saying something, and at last she managed to murmur, "I'm proud to meet you, Mrs. O'Halloran."

She had barely gotten the words out when old

Sorcha cut in with a hissing "Sh-h-h! Do not speak!" She broke off and continued to stare straight ahead with those remarkable eyes.

The musicians stopped playing and there was a long, breathless hush as everyone in the circle watched and waited.

Suddenly the old woman spoke in a voice that was strong and commanding. "Kate, 'tis the cards I need!"

The dark, handsome wife of the fiddler rose quickly from her blanket by the fire and hurried to the nearby caravan wagon. As she disappeared inside, Colum slipped into the big tent. A moment later he came out carrying a light-weight table and a small stool, but he did not take them to his great grandmother. Instead, he waited for her orders.

The old woman reached out from under the heavy folds of her cloak and took Christie's hand into hers. Her long fingers were knotted and curled in toward her palms, but with their touch Christie felt a strange vibration go through her body, almost like an electric shock.

Old Sorcha was still staring, hardly breathing, and her dark eyes looked strange, as if she were seeing a vision and trying to hold on to it, or perhaps to see more. Christie waited, motionless, hardly daring to breathe herself, her hands still locked in the old Gypsy's clasp.

Kate's footsteps on the stairs of the little wagon broke the silence. She came to her mother-in-law with a small wooden box, and old Sorcha released Christie's hand to take it.

Colum hurried to place the table in front of her,

and she put the box on top of it. Christie noticed that
both box and table were old and unpainted, but when
Sorcha opened the box it was lined with pale silk,
and the cards lay inside it.

Colum put the stool down on the side of the table
opposite his great grandmother, and motioned for
Christie to sit on it. His eyes were gleaming with
excitement.

When Christie sat down, the old woman put the
worn, frayed cards on the table and looked at her
intently. " 'Tis *you* can help me see into the future,"
she said, "by fixing your mind on the wish to know
the truth." Her voice dropped to a whisper. "We will
wish for it together, while you shuffle the cards."

Christie had shuffled cards often enough when
she'd played canasta at home with Kevin, but here
in this strange setting with the searching eyes of the
old Gypsy upon her, her hands shook and she barely
managed the task.

"Cut them into three piles, now," Sorcha whispered. "Remember 'tis only the truth we're wanting."

Trying to concentrate, Christie cut them and then
collected them again in a way that made their posi-
tions different in the pack. When she had repeated
the process twice more, the old woman took the cards
and dealt them from the top, face downward, in
what looked like the shape of a pyramid.

She turned over the first card, so that it lay face
up on the table. After she had studied it, she turned
over the second. Then she broke the silence. "The
brother—'tis he I must have!"

Kevin hurried to kneel beside Christie. "I'm here,"
he said breathlessly.

The old Gypsy gave him the same searching look she had given Christie, and then her eyes went back to the cards, and very slowly, one by one, she turned them over.

Kevin and Christie had never seen such cards before. The emblems on their faces were strange and beautiful, and they had no way of knowing what each one symbolized.

Suddenly Sorcha began to talk, but the language

she was speaking was not English, and they couldn't understand a word of it. They looked helplessly at Padraic.

"It's Gaelic," he whispered.

The unfamiliar words continued to flow from her lips, as strange and undecipherable to them as the faces of the cards. At last she stopped and sank back into her chair, her eyes closed.

"If she falls asleep now, she may never remember," Christie whispered anxiously.

Padraic gave the old woman a moment to rest, and then he said to her, "Sorcha, you spoke of what you saw in the cards, but in Gaelic, and they couldn't understand."

At the sound of his voice, she pulled herself back from the edge of sleep. For an instant, she looked at Christie and Kevin as if she had forgotten them; then her thoughts seemed to fall back into place.

" 'Tis you, Christie, who will see what no one else will see," she said softly, "and to a great treasure it will surely lead you."

"And you, lad—" Her dark eyes shifted to Kevin's face. " 'Tis with her you must be, and never leave her, for in the finding of it there will be danger."

Kevin and Christie stared at the old Gypsy, too astounded by her prophecy to speak.

She threw back her shabby hood and with her crippled fingers took hold of a silver chain and lifted it up over her head. From it dangled a shining green locket.

"Come!" she said to Christie.

Christie went to her quickly and the old woman motioned to her to kneel. Then she slipped the chain and locket down over Christie's head.

" 'Tis for you to wear it and not take it off," she commanded, though her voice was no longer strong and she seemed very tired, "but do not *open* the locket, for within it are the ashes from a sacred fire."

"Thank you," Christie murmured earnestly. "It's very beautiful—but I couldn't take it from you."

"Take it you must!" said Sorcha, forcing herself to speak powerfully again. " 'Tis the sacred ashes that will protect you wherever you go. *But do not lose it*," she warned, "for without the ashes, you will have no protection from the danger foretold in the cards."

She sank back into her chair, totally exhausted, and Padraic drew her hood up over her thin white hair.

She looked once more at Christie and Kevin. "God between you and all harm," she murmured. Then she closed her eyes and was instantly asleep.

3

The Legend of the Chalice

Kevin and Christie walked up the hill with Padraic in silence, each of them absorbed in their own thoughts about the Gypsy's prophecy. As they neared the house, a shepherd dog came running toward them, making a great show of barking while his tail wagged. Every farmhouse in Ireland seemed to have a dog on guard at the door, or sitting in a deep window sill or on a wall. They'd seen them all along the route north, dogs of all sizes and colors. This one had a long coat of light russet brown and white, and at a word from Padraic, he began to yip and prance, welcoming his master.

"I told you it might be scary," Kevin whispered while the dog continued his happy noises.

"I'm not scared," Christie whispered back, though her heart was thumping inside her chest. "How can I be scared when I've got the locket?"

"You mean you believe all that stuff about the ashes?"

"Why not?" said Christie. "You believe about the treasure, don't you?"

"I don't know," said Kevin. "If you believe that, you've got to believe in the danger, too. They go together."

"I do," said Christie, "but I'll have you and the locket to protect me."

The shepherd came to prance around them with his glad yipping.

While they petted the friendly dog, Kevin whispered to Christie and Padraic, "Let's not tell our mom the part about the danger, huh? No use worrying her."

"I won't," said Christie.

"Nor I." Padraic nodded. "It would be no help to alarm her."

When he swung open the door of his cottage, they stepped into a large comfortable room with a high ceiling that reached to the rafters, and a wash of pale rose color on the walls. At one end, a sort of stairway-ladder led up to an open loft, and at the opposite end a turf fire glowed on the hearth.

A long table was set with shining delftware, and they smelled the mouth-watering fragrance of freshly baked cake. Though they'd stopped for dinner on the way, the tantalizing odor made them suddenly hungry, and they were glad Mrs. O'Flaherty was going to serve a late Irish tea.

She was a mere wisp of a woman but she held her frail body erect in spite of her eighty-seven years. Silky white hair framed her sweet, delicate face and her eyes were a bright liquid blue, like sapphires under water. Christie slipped into her welcoming arms and there was an instant harmony between them.

The old lady greeted Kevin as if he were her own great-grandson, and when they were all seated around the table and he was drinking milk from a tall mug and eating hot buttered raisin cake, he wished he had a great-grandmother just like her.

After the first delicious bites, he and Christie couldn't contain their news any longer, and they told their mother and Mrs. O'Flaherty about Sorcha's prophecy that Christie was to find a great treasure.

"But how about that, Mom?" said Kevin. "Telling Chris she'd see something no one else would see, and then telling me to stay right with her and never leave her. What the heck do you think she would see that I wouldn't see, if I were right beside her?"

"I don't know," said Mrs. MacAlistaire, "but remember, Christie often sees things that you pass by without noticing. It all depends on what you're looking for."

"Yeah," Kevin admitted, "and on what you *imagine*. Chris imagines a lot of stuff."

"She didn't say I'd imagine anything," declared Christie defensively, "she said I'd *see* it. If it was something I imagined, how could it lead me anywhere?"

"I guess you're right," said Kevin doubtfully.

"Besides, she read it in her cards. They were amazing cards, Mommy, with all kinds of beautiful emblems and figures on them."

"They sound like tarot cards," her mother said.

"That they were," said Padraic, "the same fortune-telling cards the Romany Gypsies used in the old days."

"But that isn't all," said Christie. "I've got a surprise to show *you*, Mommy, and you too, Mrs. O'Flaherty. Look what Mrs. O'Halloran gave me." And she drew out from under her blouse the locket she had kept hidden until now. "I told her I couldn't take it, Mommy, but she insisted."

"She did, indeed," said Padraic.

Kevin and Christie were careful not to mention the purpose of the locket and Padraic was their silent conspirator.

"It's cloisonné," said Mrs. MacAlistaire, examining the green enamel fused with wire into a delicate design. "What a lovely gift!"

"That it is," said Mrs. O'Flaherty gently, "and many are the years she has worn it. It's surprised I am that she would give it away, because of what is inside it."

"That's the most mysterious part," Christie told her mother. "There are ashes in it—sacred ashes, she said."

"It's likely they are ashes from the sun fires of St. John's Eve," said Padraic.

"What are they?"

"Bonfires," said Padraic, "lighted by the people of every townland on Mid-summer's Eve, and so they have been lighted since before the writing of history. If you stand on a hill after dark, you can see them blazing up from every direction, and for each one you can count, you will have a year of good luck."

"But what makes them sacred?" Christie asked.

"It is the bone that is thrown into the fire when the flames are high," said Padraic, "the bone that represents the body of St. John. When the fire cools, the head of each family takes some of the ashes from the dying embers and keeps them to protect his loved ones from harm in the year to come."

"Then she gave us their protection," said Kevin.

"She did," said Padraic, "but it's little more than a month now until another Mid-summer's Eve."

"A lot can happen in a month," said Christie anxiously. "I think I should take the ashes back to her."

"No, you cannot," said Padraic firmly. "She would not take them. They are to guard you in the finding of the treasure."

"And I'll be there to guard you, too," said Kevin

quickly, thinking of his mother, "so what could go wrong? Golly, Mom," he went on, changing the subject, "what kind of a treasure do you think it could be?"

"H-m-m, it's hard to say," his mother said thoughtfully. "In a country like Ireland I suppose the greatest treasure would be an antiquity."

"An antiquity? What's that?"

"A relic of ancient times. Something rare and priceless because of its age."

"Like what, Mom?"

"I don't know exactly. Perhaps a monument that's been hidden or buried for thousands of years."

"Do they have things that old here?" Kevin asked in surprise.

"They do," said Padraic, "and I myself have seen them. You're right, Mrs. MacAlistaire, an antiquity it could be!"

"What have you seen?" Christie asked eagerly.

"A pagan stone," said Padraic, "right in County Galway, standing in a field with sheep grazing around it. A great boulder it is, four feet high with carvings on it made by some sculptor in ancient times."

"Isn't that the Turoe Stone?" asked Mrs. MacAlistaire.

"Turoe." Padraic nodded. "That's the name."

"I've read about it," said Mrs. MacAlistaire. "It's a ritual stone decorated with Celtic designs that date back to the second or third century before Christ."

Kevin let out a long whistle. "Wow! That's some antiquity!"

"It is," said Padraic, "and in the ruins of the monastic city of Clonmacnois, I have seen other stones with peculiar markings—grave slabs, they were, some as old as the sixth or seventh century. Could be you'd find one of those, Christie. Stumble over it, you might, in the graveyard of some ruined monastery. 'Twould be buried under a tangle of weeds and grasses, surely, and that's how you might see it when Kevin didn't. But if one of those stones should be your treasure, be careful where you step, for it might cave in under you, and you'd be in the grave itself."

"With a skeleton!" said Kevin.

"More likely several," said Padraic.

"I'd rather not find an old gravestone," said Christie, suddenly feeling a bit squeamish. "Couldn't the treasure be something else, and still be an antiquity?"

"It could," said Padraic. "Something entirely different, like the Tara brooch—or the Ardagh chalice."

"What's the chalice?" Kevin asked.

"A large silver cup with a foot and two handles," said Padraic. "A thing of beauty it was, all decorated with gold filigree and dazzling colored crystal and amber set like jewels. And the Tara brooch, a smaller relic but ornamented with designs of gold, some fine as thread and some like little ribbons, the golden wires making the shapes of beasts, and between them bright bands of amber."

"Oh, they sound wonderful!" said Christie.

"That they are, and mind you, made back in the eighth century. You can see them yourselves in the National Museum in Dublin."

"But we couldn't possibly find anything like that

now, could we?" asked Kevin.

"And why not?" said Padraic. "It's said the brooch was found in a wooden box on the bank of the River Boyne, and you'll never guess how the chalice was found."

"How?" asked Christie.

"By a boy digging potatoes!" said Padraic. "In the rath of Ardagh it was, in County Limerick just south of the Shannon Estuary where your plane came in."

"Wow!" said Kevin. "Remind me to carry a spade wherever we go!"

"It's a good idea you have there, Kevin. The boy found the chalice along with some smaller treasures inside the roots of a thorn bush. Hidden they were, under a stone slab."

"How long ago did he find them?"

"Maybe a hundred years ago," said Padraic, "but remember they were *twelve hundred* years old then. Who knows what is buried that has not yet been found? I can tell you stories of antiquities discovered behind cupboards and buried in gardens or in the peat bogs."

"You mean a brooch or a chalice could be behind a cupboard for over a thousand years and nobody'd find it?" asked Kevin in amazement.

"No, Kevin, it's not likely that's what happened. It could be the chalice was hidden by a priest in the bad times when worship was forbidden. He might have been the keeper of the treasures of his monastery. And there were hereditary keepers, members of royal families who were trusted down through the generations with keeping the treasures of their castles safe in times of war. If the life of a keeper was in danger, or if he was dying and had no one to pass them on to, he may have hidden the treasures wherever he was, and who's to say where that might have been? Or how long the treasures might lie there before they were found?"

"You must not forget, Padraic, the legend of the chalice," said Mrs. O'Flaherty.

"Which one is that, Mother?"

"The one buried beneath an O'Flaherty castle. You must tell them of that. Could be they'd find it."

"An O'Flaherty *castle*!" Kevin and Christie exclaimed in simultaneous astonishment.

"Yes," Padraic admitted quietly, "there were castles, not one, but many, long long ago."

"Holy Smoke!" said Kevin. "Why didn't you tell us?"

"Surprise number two," said his mother. "You see, the O'Flahertys were once kings of Connemara."

"*Kings*!"

"Just farmers now," said Padraic. "All that was centuries back."

"Will you tell us about it?" asked Christie.

"There is little I know," said Padraic. "Tales of the past change in the telling. And it is late now for guests who have flown six thousand miles. Too late to be talking of things that may not even be true."

"Are there any castles left?" Kevin asked.

"Yes, ruins there are."

"Could we see them?" asked Christie.

"You could, indeed, if you want to drive to the places where they stand."

"I'll say we do!" said Kevin. "Can we go tomorrow, Mom?"

"If you'll stop asking questions and finish your milk and cake so we can get to bed," said his mother with a teasing smile.

Kevin and Christie dove into the cake they'd forgotten in their excitement.

"Then I'll ask Colum to guide you," said Padraic. "He knows every place in Ireland."

"Is there really a chalice buried beneath one of the ruins?" Christie asked.

"A legend it is, Christie," said Padraic. "Who is to say whether it is true or not?"

"It's true, I think," said Mrs. O'Flaherty softly, "and maybe it is for you, Christie, that it has been waiting."

4

A Visitor in the Night

Kevin and Christie chose to sleep in the loft. The beds on each side of it were unlike any they'd ever seen before. Fitted against the slope of the rafters, they had wooden paneling extending around them on three sides and arching over them like a roof. Lying in them was as cosy as lying in a box with only one side open, and they had the added warmth of hot water bottles at their feet. For it was still early May, and they had seen snow on the mountain tops when their plane circled down to land at Shannon.

But cosy as their beds were, Kevin and Christie crept out to lie for a few minutes at the edge of the loft above the ladder-stairs, where they could look down at the turf, still burning in the fireplace.

"I wonder if I will find their chalice," said Christie dreamily. "Imagine, a cup all silver and gold with jewels on it!"

"That was the Ardagh chalice," said down-to-earth Kevin. "This one may not be so fancy."

"I'll bet it is," said Christie. "If it's buried under their castle, it must have belonged to a king."

"Just think," said Kevin, "if it hadn't been for all the wars that changed everything, Padraic, or maybe Terence, would be the king of Connemara right now!"

"And we'd be staying in a castle," Christie sighed.

"Don't be silly," said Kevin. "If they were kings, we wouldn't even know them."

"Then I'm glad they're not," said Christie, "because I like knowing them and being here in this lovely farmhouse."

"Me, too," said Kevin. "And tomorrow we'll see their castles anyway."

Staring down at the glowing turf, Kevin and Christie were sleepily conjuring up their own chosen images of treasures to be found and castles to be seen, when they were startled by a hissing sound somewhere below them.

"Phst! Phst!"

They peered down over the edge of the loft and saw the slender figure of a woman in a long night-gown and heavy shawl standing at the foot of the stair-ladder. The room was lighted only by the candle in the woman's hand, but they recognized her as Mrs. O'Flaherty.

"Christie! Kevin!" the old lady whispered. "There is something I must tell you. Come down, but softly, for it's quiet we must be. A secret thing it is, for no one else to hear."

They climbed down the ladder-stairs carefully in

the dim light, for without handrails it was a bit precarious.

"Put your backs up close to the turf," said Mrs. O'Flaherty, leading the way to the hearth. "Catch your death of colds you could, lying out of your beds like that."

She sat in a chair beside the hearth, and Kevin and Christie sat on a small rug backed up to the glowing embers of the fire.

"Do you have the locket on you?" Mrs. O'Flaherty whispered.

"Yes, I do." Christie was puzzled, but she drew the locket out from under her pajama jacket to show the old lady.

"Good. Keep it on you day and night, for if Sorcha O'Halloran gave you the locket with the sacred ashes, it was because of what she read in the cards."

"Did she tell you?" asked Kevin.

The old lady shook her head. "No, it is what I know *without* her telling."

"She said Christie would be in danger, but we didn't want to worry you or our mom."

Mrs. O'Flaherty nodded. "It's worried I am, indeed, for I myself know the danger. Many are those who have *heard* of it, but few have ever come back alive to tell of it."

"Of what?" Kevin asked sharply.

"The thing that happened to them. It was my own ancestor was taken and, thanks be to God, was brought back. A young man of eighteen he was, when it happened, and already big and strong like all the O'Farrells, but he had no power against them."

"Against whom?" Christie asked anxiously.

"The fairies!"

"The fairies!" Kevin exclaimed in astonishment, forgetting to whisper.

"Sh-h!" warned Mrs. O'Flaherty. "I can see you are doubting what I'm saying, but if you don't believe me it's carried away you may be, both of you."

The flame of the candle lighting her face revealed the distress in her liquid blue eyes.

"We do believe you," Christie insisted. "It's just that we don't know anything about fairies. What are they like?"

"Fallen angels, some say they are, and others say they are the dead returned, but it's not by looking at them that you can tell. Like any stranger, they are."

"You mean, you can't tell them from ordinary people?" asked Kevin, remembering to keep his voice hushed.

"Not at all. It's how they got Liam O'Farrell. He was walking along the shore, and two men came up from a boat. They put down a fairy mist so no one could see what happened, and then they tied him up and covered his eyes and carried him away."

"Where did they take him?" asked Christie, fascinated by the old lady's story.

"To an island beyond the Arans, far to the west-

ward. A disappearing island it is, hidden by the
fairy mists. Some say it isn't there at all, but Liam
O'Farrell knew, because he was on it himself."

"What did he say about it?" Kevin asked.

"Hardly a word," said Mrs. O'Flaherty, "and that
was one of the queer things. Kept there a week he
was, and then they brought him back and set him
down on the shore, making one of their mists. And
when he walked out of it, he was never the same
again. So it's careful you must be, speaking to
strangers. And if a mist comes down over you, pray
to the saint of the ashes, for it may be a fairy mist."

"Do they always bring a mist with them?" Christie
asked in dismay.

"No. Sometimes they come, a whole host of them,
and make a strong wind to help them in the kidnapping. Many are the people of this land who have
been stolen in their mists and their winds, and never
seen again. It's full of pranks the fairies are, and no
way of knowing what it is they will do to give a
human being trouble. Make him their slave they will,
or lead him to his death."

"Do you think it was the fairies Mrs. O'Halloran
saw in the cards?" Christie asked apprehensively.

"It's what I fear," said Mrs. O'Flaherty.

She leaned toward Christie, her face drawn with
concern. "It's not to frighten you I came, Christie
girl," she said tenderly, "but only to tell you why
it is you must wear the locket."

"I'll wear it every minute!" Christie promised.

"Then the ashes of the saint will protect you,"
said the old lady devoutly.

She rose from her chair and holding her candle

high, lighted their way up the stairs. When they reached the loft and looked down, she whispered something they couldn't hear, a blessing, perhaps. Then she tiptoed to the door of her bedroom and slipping through, closed it silently behind her.

Christie stared down at the empty room dimly lit by the last glow of the coals. "It's like a dream," she whispered, "as if she had never come at all. As if she weren't even *real*."

"She's not!" Kevin said positively. "A ghost couldn't be any farther out. All that stuff about fairies! Boy, is she wacky!"

"You shouldn't say that. You don't know anything about Ireland or what happens here."

"Don't tell me you believe that crazy story about her ancestor!" Kevin scoffed.

"I'm not sure," said Christie. She shivered suddenly, and they got into their sheltered beds and put their chilled feet on the warm hot-water bottles.

"Chris," Kevin whispered across the space between them, "you're not scared, are you?"

"No," said Christie, none too convincingly.

"Well, don't be," said Kevin, "because there are no such things as fairies, and if we get into a mist or wind, that's *all* it will be—a plain old mist and a plain old wind. Okay?"

"Okay," said Christie. But under the bedding, she closed her hand tightly around the locket and its comfort eased her into sleep.

Kevin had no need of the locket. He fell asleep promptly, but something deep inside of him was aware of his responsibility. He had always felt protective toward Christie because she was younger than he, and his sister, but this was different. This time he had been warned of a danger foreseen in the cards. Though his waking mind questioned the truth of the prophecy, even in sleep a deeper part of his mind was on guard, and he woke often during the night, alert to small sounds that he wouldn't have heard under ordinary circumstances.

Each time he dismissed them for what they were— the natural sounds of wind and rain, of branches scraping against the house—and dropped off to sleep again. But when he heard sounds inside the house, he sat up suddenly. To his surprise, he saw that it was morning.

He slipped out of bed and crept to the edge of the loft. In the room below, Padraic was kneeling before the hearth, adding chunks of turf to a newly-lighted fire. Kevin remembered that he wanted to talk to him. Padraic was a sensible man, he was sure of that, and he'd be just the person to settle all the nonsense about the fairies. Christie was still asleep, and he pulled on his bathrobe, stepped into his mocassins, and started down the stairs, moving very quietly so as not to wake her. He was halfway down when Padraic saw him.

"Ah, Kevin," he exclaimed softly, "it's up early you are, and the house still cold. I'll bring in a pot of tea to warm you up."

He was gone before Kevin could tell him that he didn't drink tea at home, and besides, he didn't want to bother him to fix something else.

Padraic returned after a moment carrying a teapot and a tray. On it was a plateful of sliced brown bread, a dish of butter and a jar of marmalade.

They sat down at the table and Kevin let him pour two steaming cups of tea, knowing the hot drink would feel good inside of him, for the fire hadn't had time to drive away the chill.

"I didn't know I'd have company this early," Padraic said with a conspiratorial smile, "and a nice surprise it is!"

They buttered their bread and Kevin spooned out a generous portion of marmalade.

"I wanted to talk to you before anybody else got up," he whispered.

"Did you now!" said Padraic. "And what about?"

Kevin hated to approach the subject so abruptly, but he didn't dare waste time. Someone might come in at any minute, worst of all, Padraic's mother. He took a sip of hot tea, and plunged in.

"Mr. O'Flaherty," he said, "there aren't really any fairies in Ireland, are there?"

"Is it the 'little people' you're thinking of?" Padraic asked.

"No, your mother said they looked just like human beings."

"So it's my mother you've been talking to."

"She came to see us in the night—"

"I don't think we were supposed to tell that," Christie cut in, in a loud whisper, from the top of the stairs. "Remember, she said it was a 'secret thing.'"

Kevin turned in surprise. "Not secret from Mr. O'Flaherty," he said defensively. "He must know about it already."

Christie put on her robe and slippers and came down the stairs. Padraic poured a cup of tea for her and she sat at the table and began to butter a slice of bread.

"What was it she told you?" Padraic asked.

"All about her ancestor, Liam O'Farrell," said Kevin. "How he was kidnapped by the fairies and then taken away to a disappearing island."

"That would be I-Brasil," said Padraic.

Christie gave her brother a look that said "I told you so!"

Kevin was incredulous. "You mean there really is such an island?" he asked.

"It's not to be found on the maps of these times," Padraic said, "but it was on some of the ancient ones. Somewhere off the coast of Connemara, they put it, out to the west of the Aran Islands. And mind you, there are those who claim to have seen it. A friend of mine says he saw it once from the westernmost point of Inishmore. And there are others who claim it comes up out of the mists once in seven years." He shrugged his shoulders. "I myself have never seen it."

"Was her ancestor really carried off by the fairies?" Christie asked.

"Now that is a question I can't answer of my own knowing," Padraic admitted. He finished his tea and refilled the cup. "It's eighty-seven years old my mother is, with eighty-seven years of memories in her head. And it could be that she has some of them mixed up, one with the other. That she had a great uncle, or maybe a great-great-uncle, named Liam O'Farrell, that I know to be true. But in the matter of the fairies, it could be she confused him with the story of a man named Morogh O'Lee."

"Who was he?" Kevin asked.

"A man kidnapped by the fairies. It happened on the coast of Ballynahinch, which used to be O'Flaherty land. Morogh O'Lee was walking along the shore when some strangers blindfolded him and took him away to the island of I-Brasil. Two days they kept him, and then brought him back. Sick, he was, for many weeks after."

"But that's just a *story*," Kevin said.

"If it's a story," said Padraic, "how would you explain the book?"

"What book?" Kevin asked in astonishment.

"The book he brought with him from the island, which he studied for seven years," said Padraic. "And after the seven years, without any other training at all, he became a doctor and practiced medicine for the rest of his life."

This was too much for Kevin to accept. "Did anybody ever *see* the book?" he asked skeptically.

"See it they did, and you yourself can see it, in the library of the Irish Academy," Padraic told him. "Called *The Book of I-Brasil* it is."

Kevin was too stunned to reply. A disappearing island drawn only on ancient maps was one thing. You could take it or leave it. But a famous book in a library in Dublin! If it was there you couldn't deny it. And named for the island, besides!

He knew what Christie was thinking, and he busied himself heaping marmalade on a fresh slice of bread to avoid her eyes. He wished she hadn't heard about I-Brasil and the books. Now she had more reason than ever to be frightened.

He didn't believe there were fairies, or even fallen

angels or ghosts, but if Morogh O'Lee and Liam O'Farrell and other people, too, had been kidnapped, then *somebody* had done it. Not having any idea who it could be made it all the more dangerous.

5

A Story of Kings

Kevin was glad when the sound of a dog barking outside changed the subject from fairies to something real, though even the barking seemed a bit odd, not quite like the dog who had greeted them last night.

"Is that your dog, sir?" Kevin asked.

Padraic was already on his feet. "It's no dog at all," he said, opening the door.

The barking was louder and closer now, and Kevin and Christie jumped up from the table and ran, a bit apprehensively, to see what it could be. There was no dog in sight, but the barking continued as if the animal were right in front of them, or else above their heads—as in fact, he was. For when they looked up they saw Ben, the crow, perched at the edge of the thatched roof, and to their amazement, it was he who was "barking." Colum was walking up the path.

"Hey, that's some imitation Ben does," said Kevin.

"It's his way of teasing the dog, and calling him, too," said Padraic, "for it's good friends they are."

Ben had stopped "barking" and was sitting with his head cocked to one side, listening.

"But it's asleep in the shed he is this morning, Ben," said Padraic, addressing the crow, "and I don't want you getting him up and making a great noise, the two of you, to wake the ladies. So be off with you, now!"

He raised his arm high and brushed the crow firmly from the roof. Ben spread his wings and circled over them.

"Go down to the meadow and visit the cows," Padraic said. "And you, Colum, get inside before he comes in with you."

"Go now, Ben," said Colum, darting in. "Take a fly around, and I'll be back with you soon."

They all stepped inside quickly and Padraic closed the door.

"It's too full of chatter he'd be, to let him come in, with the ladies still sleeping," he said.

Outside, Ben seemed to take the hint, for he flapped off toward the pastures. Padraic brought another cup for Colum and they all sat down at the table.

"Helping yourself to bread and marmalade," said Padraic, filling Colum's cup with hot tea. "There's plenty more in the kitchen."

Colum began to butter a slice of bread. " 'Tis a fine day for traveling," he said, "and I thought you might be going to see the castles."

"I hope so," said Kevin, "but we won't know till Mom gets up."

"It's sorry I am that I can't go with you, for I'm building a new barn while I have the strength of the O'Halloran men to lift the stones with me," said Padraic. "But Colum knows how to find all the old ruins as well as I do."

"You promised last night, sir, to tell us about the O'Flahertys," Kevin said.

"I know something you'll never guess," Colum bragged.

"What's that?" Kevin demanded.

"How far back their royal bloodline goes," said Colum.

"How far?" Christie asked.

"How far d'you think?" he countered.

"Five hundred years," said Christie.

"Five hundred!" Colum scoffed. " 'Tis three hundred since their castles were taken from them, and their kingship, too."

"A thousand, then," said Kevin.

"You haven't guessed it by half," said Colum importantly.

"Not *two* thousand years!" Kevin exclaimed in disbelief.

Colum nodded. "Back to the third century before Christ," he said.

"You mean there were kings in Ireland way back then?"

"There were indeed, Kevin, and long before that," said Padraic," but from the third century back, the men who write the history books disagree on what is legend and what is fact."

"Tell them about Queen Macha," Colum prompted.

"A famous queen, she was, Macha Mong Ruad, the red-haired," said Padraic, "and it is thought to be certain that she ruled in the third century B.C., though there are some who say she was a goddess. But a flesh-and-blood queen she had to be, for she founded a great stronghold told about in history to this day. Named for her it was, *Emain Macha*, and it stood against her enemies for six hundred years."

"Was she your ancestor?" Christie asked.

"Not Macha herself, but her foster son, Ugani Mor the great. Ancestor of all the royal families of three provinces, including this one. King of Ireland and of the whole of western Europe as far as the Mediterranean Sea, the ancient seanachies called him."

"Wow!" said Kevin. "Some ancestor!"

"Who were the 'seanachies'?" Christie asked, intrigued.

"The poet-historians," Padraic explained. "It was they who handed down to us the legends and the history of Ireland. Every king had his chief poet, and highly honored he was, too, next to the king himself."

"Next to the king!" Kevin was amazed.

"And no more than he deserved," said Padraic, "for to be a poet of the highest rank, he had to study no less than twelve years, and more likely twenty."

"And he had to memorize three hundred and fifty great epics," said Colum, proud of his knowledge.

"That he did," Padraic agreed. "A powerful mind he had to have, for besides the epics, he had to know all the laws and all the history of Ireland and of every important royal family in it for centuries back."

Kevin let out a long whistle.

"And that's not all of it," said Colum. "He had to be able to recite every bit of it in verse any time the king called on him—even at a moment's notice."

"I'd like to read some of the legends," said Christie.

"That you can, Christie lass," said Padraic. "Written down by the monks in the very words of the poets they were. And though the monasteries were destroyed by the invaders, and most of the great books burned or stolen, some of the precious writings were saved. And some were recited and written down again."

"That great stronghold that Queen Macha built— what was it like?" Kevin asked.

"A stone fort, I suppose it was, like the ruined ones you can still see here on the hilltops. Built in a circle they are, some of them with walls thirteen feet thick or more, and ramparts all around."

"Tell them about the royal houses inside the forts," said Colum.

"Ah, they were something to be seen, according to the poets," said Padraic. "Built of the red yew tree, they were, all the wood handsomely carved, with a front of bronze shining in the sun, and bronze shutters, too, for the windows."

"And in the center of it all, the apartments of the king and queen had a front of gold and silver, set with colored jewels," said Colum.

"Is that really true?" Kevin asked doubtfully.

"It's how the poets tell it," said Padraic, "and there were many poets telling the same things, so they could not be lying, one against the other."

"They sound like fairy palaces," said Christie dreamily.

"But real they were, and a sight to be seen, with the High King himself wearing a crimson tunic, with no doubt a brooch and a girdle of silver and gold upon him, and a torc around his neck," said Padraic, imagining the ancient scene clearly in his mind.

"What's a torc?" Christie asked.

"A sort of necklace it is, made of bands of twisted gold, and that's another kind of treasure you might find, Christie, for torcs have been dug up in recent times, in the ruins of old palaces. Or you might even find the golden girdle of a king, or his belt, set with jewels."

"Oh, I wish I might!" said Christie earnestly.

"Who was the next great king after Ugani Mor?" asked Kevin, fascinated by the long line of succession.

"Many I could tell you about," said Padraic, "but it would take a month of talking day and night. Have you heard of Cormac Mac Art?"

"No, sir."

"The greatest of the ancient kings he was, so the poets say, great in learning and wisdom. And there was Conn of the Hundred Battles—have you heard of him?"

"No sir, we don't know much about Irish history."

"A pity it is. Well, we'll skip over Cormac and Conn, but have you not heard of Niall of the Nine Hostages?"

"No, sir."

"The next great one, after Cormac, Niall was, and

there are two reasons I must tell you about him. First, for those who may say Macha and her foster son, Ugani, are more of legend than of history, I can tell you of a man who is known to be my ancestor, and no legend about it! He was Brian, the half-brother of the great Niall, and it is from him the O'Flahertys are descended surely. But it is the other reason that is more important, for it was Niall who first brought St. Patrick to Ireland."

"You mean the St. Patrick we know about in America?"

"I do—though he was no saint then, but only a hostage brought back by Niall from his expeditions in Brittany. A boy of sixteen he was, captured by the sailors of King Niall's fleet, who brought him to Ireland and sold him to an Irish chieftain. He was put to work herding sheep on a mountainside and no one to guess his destiny."

"How long was he a slave?" Christie asked.

"Seven years," said Padraic, "and it was there on that mountain, alone with his sheep, that he found God. A hundred prayers a day he said, and as many at night, and finally he had a dream that told him to escape."

"Did it work?" Kevin asked.

"It did," said Padraic. "Two hundred miles he traveled to the seacoast, and there he found a ship that carried him back to his homeland. But the country of his slavery had touched his heart, and its people had become his people, and even in his freedom he longed to be back in Ireland. And so it was that he studied for the priesthood, and when he had become a bishop, he returned to Ireland and converted the pagan land to his faith."

"We can go up north to the mountain of Croagh Patrick," said Colum eagerly. " 'Twas there St. Patrick fasted and prayed for the forty days of Lent, and from there he drove all the serpents and poisonous things into the sea."

"Is it true that there are no snakes in Ireland?" Christie asked.

"It's true. The legend tells that St. Patrick drove them into the sea forever."

"Your ancestor, Brian, the half-brother of Niall," said Kevin, "did he ever become king?"

"No, he did not," said Padraic, "but the ancestor of kings he *did* become."

"Who became the ancestor of kings?" asked Mrs. MacAlistaire cheerfully, as she opened the door of her bedroom and came out, fully dressed and ready for the day.

"Brian, the half-brother of Niall of the Nine Hostages," said Kevin. "He was the ancestor of the O'Flahertys."

"And of many other Irish chieftains, too," Padraic added.

"But perhaps no others who had a prayer about them over the gate of a famous city," said Mrs. Mac-Alistaire, her eyes glinting with mischief.

"So you've heard about that, have you?" said Padraic.

"I read about it in the guide book last night before I fell asleep," said Mrs. MacAlistaire.

"Enough to give you nightmares, wasn't it, and

you sleeping in the house of an O'Flaherty at the time," said Padraic, grinning.

"What was it, Mommy?" Christie asked, while Kevin at the same instant said, "Mom, what did you read?"

"Well," said Mrs. MacAlistaire slowly, "it seems that over the west gate of the city of Galway there used to be an inscription that read: 'From the fury of the O'Flahertys, good Lord, deliver us.' "

"Holy Smoke!" Kevin exclaimed in astonishment. "Were they really that furious?"

"They were, indeed," said Padraic.

"And were the people in the city really afraid of them?" Christie asked.

"It's true, they were because they had no right to be there," said Padraic. "They drove the Irish out of their own lands, killed Irish men, women and children and rewarded their murderers. Most of the country they took, but here and there were some chieftains who were not conquered, and beyond Galway, in the west, the O'Flahertys lived as free men. Fierce warriors they were, and many a battle was fought over the long centuries before at last the land was lost and the castles destroyed."

"Mom," said Kevin eagerly, "may we go to see the castles today?"

"I'm ready when you are," said Mrs. MacAlistaire.

"Oh, boy!" Kevin shouted, dashing for the stair-ladder. "I get the bathroom first."

"And it's a hearty breakfast I'll have on the table before you know it," said Padraic, disappearing into the kitchen, with Colum following after him.

"Mommy," said Christie, "Mr. O'Flaherty has

been telling us the most fascinating stories about his ancestors, and d'you know what?"

Mrs. MacAlistaire put her hands gently on Christie's shoulders and looked tenderly into her upturned face. "No, what?" she asked, smiling.

"He thought of some other kinds of treasure I might find, especially a king's torc! It's a sort of necklace made of gold. Wouldn't it be wonderful if I found one of those?"

"It would, darling," said Mrs. MacAlistaire, kissing Christie on the forehead.

6

Haunted Castles

When Kevin and Christie and Mrs. MacAlistaire
started out on the journey, with Colum as guide, they
had a surprising fifth passenger in the car: Ben, the
crow. Ben, it seemed, liked to travel; he was accus-
tomed to riding with Colum inside the caravan
wagons and flying out whenever he chose—and according to Colum he was more or less housebroken.
In case it was rather less than more, Mrs. Mac-
Alistaire spread paper towels over the backs of the
seats before they left.

Ben enjoyed the adventure from the first. He took
the shift from caravan wagon to car in stride, for he
had ridden in cars before when Colum hitchhiked,
and he didn't mind the sound of the motor. Without
ever losing his balance, he waddled and hopped
across the seat backs to peer out the windows on both
sides. His sharp, beady eyes took note of everything,

and frequently he made raucous crow comments on the people or creatures within his view.

Now and then, as Mrs. MacAlistaire drove north along the country roads, she had to stop the car and wait for sheep or cattle to pass. At each stop, Colum opened the window to let Ben fly out, astonishing the farmer and startling his creatures, who were nervous enough about the car, without having a crow come flapping out of it.

Ben, emerging with his sudden loud caws, had a knack of sending the sheep and cattle into a fast run, and clearing the road in a hurry. At a shout from Colum, he'd come zooming back and land on the open window. There he'd cling for a moment to screech a few final commands to the farmer and his animals, and then with a low gurgle of content at a chore well done, he'd subside on Colum's shoulder.

As the five travelers swung around the eastern end of Galway Bay, they approached the ancient city of Galway where once the inscription about the O'Flahertys had hung over the western gate.

"Are the people of this city still enemies of the O'Flahertys?" Christie asked.

"Oh, no, that was all long ago," said Mrs. MacAlistaire.

"Who were the invaders who put up the sign, Mom?" Kevin asked.

"They were the Anglo-Normans," his mother replied, "and they took the city way back in 1232 A.D."

"I bet they didn't get it without a fierce fight," said Kevin.

"I'm sure they didn't," his mother said, "but though the Irish were finally beaten, they were never really conquered, for eventually they assimilated their conquerors. The two races intermarried and the Anglo-Normans learned the Irish tongue—"

"Was that the Gaelic your great-grandmother was speaking?" Christie asked Colum.

"It was," he replied, "and Mr. O'Flaherty says they took on the Irish way of dressing, too, and the great titled lords had Irish poets in their castles."

"That's right, Colum," said Mrs. MacAlistaire, "and they even changed their English and Norman names to Irish names, until at last the invaders were said to be more Irish than the Irish themselves."

"And now they're all Irish together," said Christie.

"Yes," said her mother, "and County Galway is part of the Republic of Ireland."

"With all the kings gone," said Kevin regretfully.

"But not the castles," said Christie.

They crossed the Corrib River and, skirting the city, swung to the northwest and out to the open country of farms and bog and moorland.

"It's not long now you'll have to wait," said Colum.

"You mean we're really coming near to a castle of the O'Flahertys?" asked Christie, hardly daring to believe it.

"Two of them we're near," said Colum, "but I'll not be taking you to the first."

"Why not?" asked Kevin.

"Because it's killed we might be if we went there," said Colum, a note of fear in his voice.

"Killed!" Christie gasped in astonishment.

"By the stones that do fly through the air, and nobody there to be throwing them."

"Then how come they fly through the air?" Kevin demanded.

"It's said it's the gatekeeper."

"But you said 'nobody there'—"

"No living man," said Colum. "He's been dead for a thousand years."

"You mean the castle has a ghost?" asked Christie, with a slight shiver of excitement.

"Ghosts there are, surely, in every old castle in Ireland," Colum replied. "Some are seen and some are heard, but few are as evil as this one."

"What did he do?" Kevin asked.

"Collected a toll, they say, from every person, rich or poor, who passed by on the road, but even after they'd paid it, he was likely as not to kill them by breaking their backs with the rocks he threw after them."

"Why did he do that?" Kevin asked.

"For the mere sport of it, to test his aim and his strength," said Colum.

Christie felt a chill of horror run down her spine. "If the O'Flahertys owned the castle, why did they have such a wicked man at their gate?" she asked.

"One of themselves he was," said Colum, "or at least half of him was O'Flaherty, it's said. And half-gone in the head he was, too, with the strength of ten men in him. But finally he met his match and got himself killed in a horrible way—too horrible to speak of in front of a lady and a girl."

"That's quite a story, Colum," said Mrs. Mac-Alistaire. "Where did you hear it?"

"From my great-grandmother," said Colum. "But

all the Gypsies have heard it, and the people who live beyond the bogs roundabout. They've seen the rocks flying and know who's throwing them. They can tell you I haven't made it up."

"I'm sure you haven't," said Mrs. MacAlistaire.

"Does Padraic know about it?" asked Kevin.

"He does, to be sure."

"Does he believe it?" asked Christie.

"How would he know, and it happening a thousand years ago?" asked Colum. "There were good O'Flahertys and bad, he says, and who's to know the truth or the lie of the story about the gatekeeper?"

"Then how can you be scared of an old legend and a man dead a thousand years?" asked Kevin.

"Legend or not, it's scared I am," said Colum, "for my own people tell of a Gypsy boy who dared to enter that gate and was found dead the morning after. A broken back he had, and not a mark on him. But his eyes were popped half out of his head from the sight he saw before he died."

"And you think it was the ghost of the gatekeeper?" asked Kevin.

"Who else would it be, and his back broken in the very same spot as all the gatekeeper's victims before him?" asked Colum. "A tinker boy of my own tribe he was, and that's enough for me. If you want to go into that castle, I'll tell you the way, but you'll have to stop and let me out of the car now, and Ben and I will wait right here until you get back—*if* you get back at all."

"I don't think there's any doubt we'd get back, Colum," said Mrs. MacAlistaire.

"I don't want to go there, Mommy," said Christie

emphatically, poking her elbow into Kevin's ribs. His eyes met hers.

"Okay, let's skip it," he said, and his look told her he was recalling what the old Gypsy had said about the danger.

Colum was silent, and she guessed that he was thinking of it, too. Even Ben the crow sat on the back of the front seat, peering at her with his keen black eyes, as if he sensed something in the air.

Christie fumbled inside her sweater. The locket with the sacred ashes was hanging from its silver chain around her neck. She took it into her hand and held it tightly. Ben's eyes were still upon her, watching her every move.

"We'll be coming to the second one soon," said Colum, out of the silence. "Aughnanure it is, and the best of the O'Flaherty castles still standing. I'll tell you when to be turning off the main road."

"Does this one have a ghost, too?" asked Kevin.

"It does," said Colum, "but you won't be seeing it."

"You can bet on that!" Kevin said, with a grin.

"You can, indeed," Colum snapped back, "but only because you have no blood of the O'Flahertys in you. If you did have, you'd be seeing it, whether you wanted to or not!"

He pointed to a side road, just ahead. "We'll be turning there, Ma'am, to the right," he told Mrs. MacAlistaire.

She followed his instructions, and they turned onto a road leading toward Lough Corrib, the large lake that emptied into the Corrib River, which carried its waters into Galway Bay.

"Has Padraic seen the ghost?" Christie asked.

"He has," said Colum.

"Who is it?" asked Kevin. "One of his ancestors?"

"It is."

"How often has he seen it?" Christie asked.

"Twice," said Colum. "Twice he has come to Aughnanure, once as a boy and once as a man, and both times he has seen it. He will not be coming again, he says, for to be seeing the dreadful sight over and over is enough to make any sane man demented."

Kevin was intrigued. "What kind of a 'dreadful sight' is it?" he asked.

"I don't rightly know," Colum admitted, "but I have made a guess."

What that guess was, Kevin didn't discover, for at that moment Christie cried, "There it is!"

Some hundred yards ahead of them he saw a massive tower of stone, its dark gray walls rearing up against a clouded sky.

"Wow!" said Kevin. "That's some castle!"

"Six stories high," said Colum, "and in some places you can still see the two bawns."

"What are 'bawns'?" asked Kevin, puzzled.

"Walls they are, high and stout, that surround the courtyard of the castle. Most have only one, but Aughnanure has two."

The base of the tower was hidden from their view by the house and outer buildings of a small farm, so that Aughnanure appeared to be behind it, in a back pasture. As they drove closer, they saw that the farm was fenced in, its gate locked, and signs proclaimed that this was private property, not to be violated by trespassers.

"They've got us shut out!" Kevin exclaimed with shock.

"But they can't do that," Christie protested. "It's the O'Flahertys' castle."

"Not since the war at the close of the seventeenth century," said Mrs. MacAlistaire. "That's when they were finally dispossessed."

"Then you mean this farmer owns it?" Christie asked, in distress.

"I don't know, dear," said her mother. "According to the guide book, many of the greatest antiquities of Ireland are out in someone's cow pasture."

"But we have to get in!" Christie insisted. "Mrs. O'Flaherty told us the chalice was buried beneath the wall of their castle."

"Remember that's only a legend," her mother warned, "and even if it were true, we don't know which castle."

Christie's thoughts raced back to the first castle— the one with the rocks that flew through the air, propelled by the ghost of the horrible gatekeeper. If they couldn't get into Aughnanure, the very thing she had dreaded might happen: they might have to go there to find the treasure.

"We'll not be kept out!" Colum declared audaciously. "Drive on, Ma'am, and I'll find a way to get in."

Mrs. MacAlistaire drove on down the road until they had passed the farmhouse and suddenly, across a stretch of soggy pasture, they saw the castle in full view.

It stood on a crag, and the dark gray stones of its ramparts seemed to rise right out of the rock. A little river flowed around its base, and in the bawn above it there were narrow slits that must once have been used for guns. Beyond the high protective walls, they could see only the "keep" of the castle, the tower-part of it that rose six full stories to the battlements. It was a great rectangular fortress with tall narrow windows facing to the four winds at each story. At two of its corners about halfway up the tower, round turrets jutted out from the wall, and they, too, had gun emplacements.

Yet strong though the fortress looked, Christie thought, somehow it had been taken by the enemy.

"There's no fence between us and the river, and there're no signs, either," said Kevin. "Stop here, Mom, and let's go!"

"You three go," said his mother, as she shut off the motor and set the brakes. "You *four*, I mean," she added, acknowledging Ben with a grin, "and if you find a way to get inside, signal me and I'll come."

"Okay," Kevin agreed, opening the car door with an exuberant burst. An instant later, he was racing Colum and Christie across the pasture. But Ben had already flown to the top of the ramparts and now stood cawing raucously, as if to brag about his superior talents.

"Shut up, you stupid bird," Colum hissed in a loud whisper, "or you'll be betraying us to the farmers and yourself to the big gray crows hereabouts."

Ben didn't get the point. Instead, he seemed to catch the note of excitement in Colum's voice, for he responded with a whole repertoire of shrieks and cackles, as if he were absolutely delighted with the promise of adventure.

"Hist, you demented creature!" Colum whispered again insistently. "It's thrown out we'll be before we even get in, if you keep that up. Hist, now, hist!"

This time Ben seemed to sense the urgency in Colum's voice, for he stood silently on the wall, peering down with his head cocked at an inquisitive angle, and listening.

"That's a fine bird," Colum whispered approvingly. "Good Ben, smart Ben."

Ben blinked his eyes, relishing the praise.

"And you'd better be keeping your beak shut the whole time," Colum warned, "or those gray crows will come and get you, surely."

"Will they really?" Christie whispered.

"They will, indeed," said Colum. "It's big they are

and mean, and they don't like one of Ben's breed and him the pet of a man."

Ben made a guttural comment and then took off in a wide, spiraling flight toward the battlements, as if he were going up to stand lookout for enemies.

Kevin watched him enviously. "He may be the only one of us to get up there," he said.

They were standing on the river bank in lush green grass overlaid with white and yellow wildflowers, but there was no bank on the opposite side, for the river undercut the rock of the crag, and the walls rose high and sheer above it. Nor was there a bridge.

"How did the O'Flahertys get into it?" Christie asked.

"The river was nowhere to be seen when they were building Aughnanure," said Colum. "Running underground it was, with nobody suspecting it. But they found it soon enough when it came up in the middle of their castle, and the whole great banquet hall fell into the water."

"*Fell in!*" Kevin and Christie exclaimed almost simultaneously.

"And they giving a grand banquet at the time," said Colum.

"A banquet," said Christie thoughtfully. "If there were royal guests present, wouldn't they have been drinking out of gold and silver chalices?"

"They would indeed," said Colum, his green-gold eyes glinting with excitement. "There's at least one big wall of the hall still left standing—on the far side of the keep."

"Then we've got to get in," Kevin declared decisively, "even if we have to ford the river and scale the wall!"

"I think there's a little footpath farther on, along the bank," said Christie.

"I see it," said Colum. "A cow path, no doubt, and leading straight to the farmer's stable."

"Let's try it, anyway," said Kevin, starting toward it.

They walked silently in single file, following the river as it rolled along at the edge of the crag. Colum had been right. The path did lead to the farmer's back fence and another locked gate. But for the moment, at least, there was no one in sight in house or barnyard. And better still, at that point the river curved away from the fenced-in land to swing in a wide arc beneath a natural stone bridge and disappear inside the castle walls.

The top of the bridge was well above them, and there was barely foot space between the corner fence post and the river, but they maneuvered it without slipping into the water and went on to scramble up the steep embankment.

Colum reached the bridge first. "Hurry!" he whispered, "before anyone comes!"

They ran across the bridge only to be confronted by another barrier: a gate that stretched from one side of the high bawn to the other. It had no lock, but it was wired shut.

"They're not keeping us out with any old wire!" Kevin declared with determination, as he worked to unfasten it.

After a few moments of nervous suspense, he

swung the gate open, they stepped through, and he wired it closed behind them. They were inside the high stone walls now, standing where once Irish kings had walked. They paused, each of them feeling a change of mood, a sense of the past, of people long dead, and events sorrowful and sinister.

Christie's heartbeat quickened, and she felt an inner excitement, and expectancy—but also a fear. Old Sorcha's prophecy made it impossible to feel one without the other.

7

A Ghost and a Thief

The three of them stood facing the great stone rectangle of the tower, which seemed to stare back at them with two narrow slits of eyes. The tall mullioned windows were the only openings in the thick stone walls. There was no entrance in sight.

"It's at the other end of the keep we'll find the door," said Colum. Though they were safely inside the ramparts, he was still speaking in a whisper, and Kevin and Christie felt the same blend of awe and apprehension. They waited for him to lead the way, but instead he said, "It's you that should be going first, Christie, for it's you that is to see what no one else will see."

Christie looked down the long stretch of courtyard that was like a gray corridor between the high wall on one side and the massive tower on the other, and hesitated, remembering Colum's story of the

O'Flaherty ghost, a spirit still lingering somewhere within the keep, invisible—but waiting.

"Go now," Colum urged, "for I wouldn't feel right to be going ahead of you, and you the one that's to be finding the treasure. But I'll be warning you both of one thing," he went on. "Letting you go first is the best I'll do for you, for if I myself see a treasure, it will be my own, surely, and I'll not be sharing it at all."

"That's fair enough," said Kevin. "Finders keepers!"

Christie summoned her courage and led the way, moving soundlessly on rubber-soled shoes. As she neared the end of the corridor between wall and tower, she stopped suddenly and with a silent but emphatic gesture, warned the boys to stop behind her.

From where she stood, a new scene opened up before her: a grassy pastureland flecked with wildflowers and bounded on the far side by two high stone bawns, one some distance beyond the other. In the center of the pasture, out of view of the boys, was the sight that had startled and delighted her: a white mare lying in the green grass nuzzling her foal.

As Christie stood motionless, the mare became aware of her and lifted her head to stare at her with great black eyes, her ears cocked alertly. The foal lay beside her, his coat fawn-colored, his little mane and tail dark, his upraised head and neck clearly outlined against the broad white shoulders and neck of his mother. He was so small and perfect that Christie hardly dared breathe for fear her presence would make him take flight.

The mare's steady gaze caught the foal's attention, and he turned his head toward Christie, his little dark ears pricked, his wide brown eyes meeting hers without fear. It was then she saw that he had a blaze of white the length of his face from his forehead to his tiny dark muzzle.

She longed to move quietly toward the mother and infant, but just then Colum and Kevin crept up to stand beside her, and the mare saw them. She got to her feet with a swift heave of her big body, her black nostrils flaring, and a glint of fire in her eyes. She stood for an instant, white and immense beside her foal, and then with a snort she started for them.

"Run for it! She's coming after us!" Colum hissed, and he fled toward the entrance of the castle, with Christie and Kevin right behind him.

The great oak door was open, and when they had rushed inside, Colum slammed it shut and leaned his weight against it.

"Lean with me," he commanded, "for she might be trying to come in. This might be her stable!"

They stood beside him, putting their weight against the door to hold it shut, and heard the mare snort and paw the ground on the other side.

"Listen to that!" said Colum apprehensively. "A wild one she is. Did you see the fire in her eyes?"

"She didn't mind me," said Christie regretfully. "She looked very gentle—"

"—until she spotted us!" Kevin cut in. "Then, wow!"

"Three strangers were too many," Christie said defensively, "and she was protecting her foal. Did you see how beautiful he was?"

"Two days old," said Colum expertly, "or maybe three. But did you see the size of her? Born of a water stallion she could be."

"What's a water stallion?" Kevin asked.

"*Each uisce*—a sea creature—and if he mates with a land-mare, it's a horse of great size and strength their foal will be, but of a strange nature, surely."

"In what way?" Kevin asked.

"With the size of her and the fire, she could be one," said Colum, "and if she is, she will stay on land until someone offends her, and then she may gallop off to live under the sea."

"Wow, you're as wacky as the old lady," said Kevin. "She's just an ordinary mare protecting her colt, and she didn't like us."

"I hope we didn't offend her," said Christie, letting herself be carried away by the fantastic idea. "I wouldn't want her to gallop off into the sea and abandon that adorable foal."

"It's lucky we'd be if she did," said Colum, "for it could happen she won't let us out of here."

"Listen!" said Kevin. "I think she's going away."

Outside, they heard retreating hoofbeats.

"But where?" asked Christie anxiously. "Look and see."

"For gosh sake, Chris!" said Kevin in exasperation as he opened the door a crack and peered out. "She's trotting off to the other end of the pasture and the colt's running with her. And she's no supernatural horse, so snap out of it!"

"It's little you know about Ireland," said Colum mysteriously.

"I know one thing: you're all too far out for me,"

said Kevin. "And now that we're inside the castle, I'm glad I'm not an O'Flaherty so I won't have to see their ghost."

"Have I said there'd be no others?" asked Colum, deliberately provoking Kevin. "It's near five hundred years old this keep is, and who's to say how many there are haunting it?"

"Okay, then let them show themselves," said Kevin, boldly taking up the challenge. "I'll believe in them when I see them and not before."

"Kevin!" Christie whispered in alarm.

"She's right," said Colum, his voice hushed. "You're asking for it, and could be you'll get more than you asked."

"I'm ready!" Kevin declared confidently.

He strode from the entry into the huge room that was the lower floor of the keep, and for the first time since they'd closed the door against the white mare, they all turned and looked at it. It was cold and gloomy and its thick walls arched up two stories to taper, stone on stone, into the vault of the ceiling.

But for the pale light slanting in through its few windows, Christie thought, it might have been a dungeon where men had suffered and died. She shook off the image. It had not been a dungeon, surely, but the first floor of a castle in which the ancestors of Padraic and Terence had lived; yet the atmosphere of the room was brooding and ominous, as though some sorrow or terror of the past still lingered in the dark gray stone.

Kevin was standing in the middle of the room, staring up into the shadowed vaulting above him.

"That'd be a good place for ghosts to hang out," he said jauntily, "but I don't see any. If they're going to come out they'd better get to it, because I haven't got time to hang around waiting."

"Don't say that!" Christie whispered. "One of them might put a curse on you."

"Curses are put on by *living* people," said Kevin, "not by ghosts."

"But it's their ghosts that carry them out," said Colum nervously, "and with us here helpless, not knowing what curses there may be on this place or what to look out for, it's you I'm telling to be careful, Kevin MacAlistaire, before you bring down something dreadful upon us all."

"Could there be curses on a *castle*?" asked Christie anxiously.

"There could," said Colum, "and on every person that would be coming into it. Many enemies the O'Flahertys had, surely, for it's mighty chieftains they were, once ruling not only Connemara, but all of Galway and the seacoast lands of Sligo and Donegal and even farther north. And their great power made other men jealous and full of hate."

"Even if there were curses on the castle," said Kevin briskly, "they'd have nothing to do with us."

"What did the gatekeeper's ghost have to do with the Gypsy boy killed by his stone? Tell me that!" said Colum. "And many more are the tales I've heard of other castles and ghosts in them whose way of killing a man would make the dying from a rock thrown at your back seem easy. Horrible ghosts they are, in castles where it's said the ceilings still drip with blood at night, and it runs red down the stone stairways."

Christie shuddered and looked up, involuntarily, at the vaulted ceiling.

"There's nothing up there, Chris," said Kevin firmly. "No ghosts, no blood—"

"Please, Kevin, don't say any more!" Christie pleaded.

"I'm just trying to keep you from being scared."

"You're only making it worse."

"You're letting all these wild stories of Colum's get to you."

"It's more than that," said Christie, her voice faint. "It's what I feel—"

Kevin came to her side quickly. "Chris, you okay?"

"Yes—"

"Then what do you feel?"

"Something about this room—"

"Is there anything you're *seeing*?" asked Colum, his eyes searching hers.

"No—but there's a heaviness. I feel it pressing—" She put her hand to her throat. "It's like a pain in my throat and chest."

She saw a change in Colum's eyes—a look of surprise and alarm. "You *know* something," she said. "Something about this room."

"It's wrong you are," he insisted. "There's nothing I know I've not told you."

"It's about the ghost Padraic saw," said Christie.

"But he's never said what it was," Colum reminded her.

"You had an idea. You said you'd made a guess."

"A guess is all it was," said Colum, "and I'd not be telling it to you here."

Christie stared at Colum, holding his eyes. They told her what his lips denied, that his "guess" had some connection with what she was feeling.

"I want to get out of here!" she said, with a sudden turn toward the door.

"No, wait—don't go!" Colum protested, catching her by the arm and spinning her around to face the room again. "You're to *see* something," he said. "It's for the treasure you've come here, remember? But first, my great-grandmother said you'd be seeing something nobody else would see. And by not looking, you've given yourself no chance."

"I don't want to look!" Christie cried. "I want to get out of this room!"

"There's nothing to see here, anyway," said Kevin, taking hold of her other arm. "It's just a bare, deserted room. Let's go upstairs."

He pulled her free of Colum's grasp and led her through an archway in a wall near the door by which they had entered. The wall was thick and circular in shape, almost like a tower inside the corner of the keep, and within it the stairway spiralled up from ground level to the battlements on the roof. A narrow slit of window admitted enough light to let them see the steep stone steps which were barely wide enough for a man's foot at one end, and tapered to nothing at the other. Kevin and Christie had seen modern spiral stairways made of steel, but they were amazed that these castle stairs could have been built of stone to rise six stories and more, hundreds of years ago.

They started up, with Colum hot on their heels.

"Let's go all the way to the roof now," said Kevin enthusiastically.

"Okay," said Christie, relieved at the thought of getting out of the dark, oppressive keep and into the open air.

They paused for breath at the little turret that jutted out at the corner of the third floor. Here men-at-arms had stood watch day and night, guarding the castle against attack.

Kevin peered out of a gun emplacement. "I can see what's left of the two bawns from here," he said. "They both had turrets at the southwest corners."

Christie peered through another opening and saw the white mare grazing peacefully inside her pasture walls, while her foal bent his little head beneath her belly to nurse. She yearned to go back down to them, but Kevin was already racing up the spiral stairs, and she followed him with Colum right behind her.

Their footsteps echoed in the stone stairwell, and they ran without stopping all the way to the roof. As they emerged, gasping, Ben greeted them with jubilant caws of welcome from a chimney top, and then swooped down to land on Colum's head and none too gently peck and nibble at his curly red mop of hair.

The wind was strong and chill, but after the gloom of the castle the air seemed fresh and sweet, and for the first time they could see across the trees of the adjoining land to the wide blue stretch of Lough Corrib and its small islands.

But Colum had only one thing on his mind. With an impatient gesture, he brushed Ben from his head and ran to the south battlement.

"Christie," he called, "it's from here you can see it."

Christie and Kevin came to stand beside him, and Ben landed on the parapet and moved toward them with his swaggering little walk.

"Down below us it is," said Colum, pointing. "The one wall left standing, and the river coming in and taking away all the rest."

"You mean that was the banquet hall?" asked Kevin.

"And a grand one, surely," said Colum, nodding.

Far below them, a thick stone wall rose up out of the green pasture. At the end nearest them, they could see a fine archway and along the length of the wall there were several handsome arched windows. But for all its thickness, it had been broken off at both ends as if by a giant's hand, and the rest of the building had been swallowed up or carried away.

The wall now stood alone on what remained of the crag on which it had been built, for the crag, too, had been split asunder, and a part of it had caved in, allowing the river to rise to the surface.

Now the river flowed in a wide, placid curve through what had once been the banquet hall. Its eastern bank was the steep, shattered stone of the crag; its opposite shore, a low, moist pasture edged with trees. There were ducks and geese swimming idly on the surface of the dark green waters, but they stayed well above the small rapids, where the river slid downslope.

"Hey!" said Kevin suddenly. "What happens to the river? It disappears."

"It does," said Colum. "Goes right back where it came from."

"You mean underground?"

"I do. Right under the crag. And down there from the lower shore, you can see it happen."

"Say, we forgot to signal Mom," said Kevin. He crossed to the battlement on the opposite side and waved silently until he got his mother's attention, then, with a gesture, indicated the approach she should take.

Ben had hopped over to stand beside Christie, and now he was peering at her as he had done before, in the car. Colum noticed it.

"Taken a liking to you Ben has," he said, "or else —" he added on second thought—"or else it is that he knows something. A strange bird he is." He looked thoughtfully from Ben to Christie. "Let's go down," he said, "for it could be you'd see something where the river goes under."

Christie was glad to break away, for Ben's intent stare disturbed her. She intended to run down the six flights of the keep even more swiftly than she had run up, but she had reached only the fourth floor when Kevin and Colum caught up with her.

"Wait, Chris!" Kevin pleaded. "We're missing the whole thing. I want to see the castle."

"Then *you* see it," Christie said. "I'll wait outside."

"No, you've got to stay with me," Kevin insisted, gripping her arm. "Remember, old Sorcha said I was never to leave you. That means you can't leave me either."

"It's you that's wearing the locket," said Colum, blocking her way. "It's safe you are, surely, with the sacred ashes on you and us to protect you."

With her escape cut off, Christie let them lead her

from the stairway into another great hall, and it, too, was vaulted as the lower one had been.

"It was here on the top floors the chieftains lived with their families," Colum said. "Safer they were, to be high up, with the soldiers and servants staying below."

"Boy, these huge rooms must have been something when they were fixed up with furnishings fit for a king," said Kevin.

For a moment, Christie let herself imagine the rich furnishings that must have adorned the hall when the O'Flahertys lived there: long tables, deep chests and high cupboards, and royal chairs and benches, all of fine heavy woods and elaborately carved by hand; rich old tapestries and beautiful paintings, and all manner of decorative pieces— statues and chalices of gold and silver. Her mind lingered on the legendary lost chalice, but the whole image of the room darkened as the feeling of gloom overtook her again.

The same melancholy sense of the past seemed to fill this hall, as it had the one below. Only here her emotions were more intense, and she felt closer to whatever had happened. Something cruel, she thought, some evil deed committed in hate. Her heart felt heavy, and the pressure on her throat returned.

Kevin and Colum were exploring adjoining rooms and passages, and she turned to run out of the hall, when suddenly a sound stopped her. She stood riveted to the spot, holding her breath as she listened. The sound came again, unquestionably clear and recognizable: the wild, tearing sobs of a woman.

Stunned, Christie stood listening while the sobs

subsided into a low moaning, as though the woman were exhausted by her sorrow, and then wrenched by her anguish, she began again with the desperate weeping. Christie fumbled for the locket, and holding it tightly in her hand, she pivoted in a slow circle, her heart pounding wildly and her breath withheld. The sobbing was all around her, and she felt ghostly eyes upon her, but she saw nothing.

It was then that Kevin and Colum returned. Kevin took one look at his sister's pale, stricken face and demanded, "What is it, Chris? What's happened?"

"Sh-h!" she whispered. "Listen!"

Motionless, the two boys stood, listening. The cycle began again: the moaning and then the sobbing.

After a moment, Kevin said, "Listen to what?"

"You mean you can't hear it?" Christie asked with unbelief.

"Hear what?" asked Colum.

"The sobbing," said Christie desperately. "The terrible heartbroken sobbing!"

The boys listened again, and Christie watched them, knowing they weren't hearing what she was hearing.

"It's the wind," Kevin said. "That's what it is: the wind moaning through all the cracks and gun holes."

"It's not," said Christie impatiently. "Don't you think I know the difference between the sound of the wind and a woman crying?"

"Much the same they could be," said Colum. "But do you *see* her?"

"No."

"Have you looked close?" he asked intensely. "Remember, it's the *seeing* that counts."

"I can't see her, but she's here. Something happened to break her heart, and that's what I've been feeling in this keep."

"You're imagining it, Chris," said Kevin gently. "It's the wind you hear. It does sound sort of like a person crying."

"It's a ghost," Christie insisted, almost in tears herself. "It's the ghost of a heartbroken woman!"

She turned and fled down the stairs, but the sobbing was still with her. Now it seemed, in fact, to be coming up the stairs toward her.

At the foot of one flight, Christie changed her course and ran into the third-floor room, and there the sobbing seemed to be coming from the huge hearth, as if the invisible woman were kneeling there.

As Kevin and Colum ran into the room, Christie said, "She's right here on the hearth. Can't you hear her now?"

"It's the wind," said Kevin patiently. "Stop and think, Chris, and you'll know it's the wind coming down the chimney."

But Christie was sure of what she was hearing. Still clasping the locket desperately, she eluded the two boys and ran down the stairs, gasping, half-sobbing, until she reached the heavy oak door. Pulling at it with one hand while she pressed the locket to her chest with the other, she flung it wide and rushed out of the haunted castle and into the open pasture.

Ben saw her and glided down to land on the wall of the ruined banquet hall, where he stood above the archway cawing an excited stream of crow greetings.

In her frantic flight, Christie had forgotten the

mare and her colt, but now she saw that the talkative crow and perhaps her own agitated exit from the keep had startled the mare, and she was moving to- ward her. The look in her black eyes was less aggres- sive than questioning, and the foal moved with her, his little head upraised. Secure beside his mother, he seemed unafraid, but Christie knew that if the boys came running out behind her, the mare's attitude would change instantly, as it had before.

She started toward mare and foal, her hands out- stretched in a gesture of welcome, while she spoke in a low crooning voice. Reassured, the mare seemed to be coming to meet her, the expression in her eyes gentle and friendly.

Suddenly Ben dove like a black streak toward Christie, as if he were going to attack her. Instead, he swept down to the ground at her feet, and then took off with a burst of speed, but not before she saw the gleam of the silver and green locket in his beak.

In a flash, she realized what had happened: in the castle she had been holding the locket so tightly that without realizing it, she had broken the delicate silver chain. When she had let go of it to reach her hands out to the mare and foal, it had fallen to the ground. And now Ben was soaring up into the sky, delighted with his thievery.

Forgetting the mare, Christie shouted at him desperately, "Ben, come back! *Ben!*"

The boys burst out of the keep.

"What is it?" Kevin called. "What's the matter?"

"Help me!" Christie cried. "Ben has the locket. I've got to get it back!" She cut across the pasture and through the archway, trying to follow Ben, who

had flown over the wall and was circling in a wide
arc above the broken crag and the river.

Alarmed by the hubbub, the mare started after
the boys with a warning snort, and they raced
through the archway, escaping by inches as she
reached out to nip them. She paused in the arch,
nearly filling it with her breadth, while the boys fled
to the brink of the shattered crag. It was obvious that
she could have followed, but perhaps she knew the
sheer drop at the edge spelled danger for her foal,
for she stood pawing the ground and snorting to
indicate that the wall was a boundary they'd better
not cross again.

Oblivious of the mare, Christie was calling and
pleading with Ben, while she ran along the length of
the crag, trying to stay under him as he flew overhead. The boys, too, began to shout at him, Colum
alternately threatening and cajoling him in Gaelic.

Excited by so much attention, Ben began to show
off, diving and somersaulting down toward them and
then flapping up and out over the river in an aerial
exhibition.

For Ben it was all pure joy, and high above the
water he opened his beak to let out an exuberant
"Caw!" The locket fell toward the river, and while
Christie and the boys gasped in horror, Ben dove
under it and miraculously caught it in time. But his
hold on it must have been insecure or uncomfortable,
for he tried with one foot to adjust it and instead
dropped it beyond his recovery. As he made a futile
dive, it fell into the deepest part of the river.

Christie stared, appalled, into the depths where
the locket had fallen.

"It's gone," she murmured, "and our protection is gone with it."

"Maybe not," Kevin said. "Maybe there's a way to get it back."

Colum was shouting skyward at Ben, scolding him soundly in Gaelic, while the crow circled high above the water, his keen eyes searching for his stolen treasure.

"I wish he were a cormorant," said Kevin. "Then he could dive down and get it himself."

They were standing at the brink of the crag, where it dropped off a precipitous ten feet or more into the river.

"Can you see it?" Kevin asked.

"No," said Christie, "and I haven't taken my eyes off the place where it went down, but the water is dark, and it's a sort of maroon-color at the bottom."

"Probably a layer of silt, and the locket's sunken into it," said Kevin. "That's why we can't see it. But you keep your eyes on the exact spot, and I'll go in after it."

"Oh, no!" Christie cried, turning to him in protest.

"You took your eyes off it!" Kevin exploded in annoyance. "Now you've lost it!"

"No, I haven't," said Christie, turning back to the river. "But you musn't go in. It's too dangerous!"

"Don't waste time arguing," said Kevin, stripping off his sweater and shirt. "I've got to get to it, in case the current might carry it away. Have you found the spot again?"

"I think so," said Christie, though it was hard now to be sure of any one place in the dark flowing breadth of the river.

"Don't take your eyes off it again," he commanded. "I won't be able to stay in long. That water's ice cold."

"Too cold!" Christie insisted, not daring to look up. "You could get cramps."

Kevin had stepped out of his shoes and socks and was stripping off his pants. Colum turned from his berating of Ben to see Kevin standing in his shorts at the brink of the crag.

"What is it you're doing?" he asked in astonishment.

"Going in for the locket," said Kevin, matter-of-factly.

"But it's paralyzed you'll be from the cold and carried underground to drown!" Colum protested.

"Please, Kevin, don't go in!" Christie pleaded, raising her eyes.

"You looked up!" Kevin shouted. "Now you've lost the place again!"

"All right, I've lost it," said Christie stubbornly. "Now I can't tell you where it was, so there's no point in going in!"

But Kevin knew how distressed she was about the loss of the locket, and he was already letting himself down over the broken edge of the crag. For the first few feet, jagged spurs of stone jutted out to give him hand and footholds, but below that the rock receded inward, and he had no choice but to drop directly into the river.

"Find the spot, Chris!" he called, and letting go, he plunged down into the maroon-green depths. For a moment, his head went under and then he surfaced, gasping from the cold.

"Where?" he demanded.

"Out toward the middle," Christie directed, and he stroked toward the center of the river.

"That's far enough!" she called, and he turned, treading water.

"Upstream or down?" he yelled.

"Down a little," she answered.

He swam a few strokes with the current.

"About there!" Christie shouted.

"Okay!" He filled his lungs and jack-knifed under.

Christie and Colum watched tensely. No more than fifteen yards beyond the point of Kevin's dive, the river surged into a wide tunnel of rock and disappeared into its underground passage. When he surfaced again, the current had carried him closer to the cave-like opening.

"No luck!" he shouted. "It's dark down there!" And then, sucking in air, he jack-knifed again.

After a long moment, he came up, gasping.

"Kevin, come back!" Christie called. "I don't care about the locket. Just come back!"

When he could speak, he shouted, "I think I saw it, lying on top of a stone!"

While he filled his lungs, Christie warned, "Look out for the cave! You're drifting closer!"

He dove under and Christie waited with Colum, her heart hammering in her chest, while unconsciously she held her breath as her brother was holding his. They could see him dimly, and his body was going with the current toward the tunnel.

Christie let out her breath and took in air, but Kevin was still under, and it looked as if he were swimming right into the mouth of the cave. She and

Colum ran along the bank, following him. It seemed impossible that he could stay under so long.

He lunged up suddenly, gasping in air, and dove down just short of the opening, while Christie screamed, "Kevin!"

The current was swift as the river rushed into the tunnel, and the space between the rock and water was less than two feet. If Kevin lunged up again, he could smash his head against the top of the cave.

His body disappeared into the darkness, and Christie screamed his name frantically, knowing that he couldn't possibly hear her.

Suddenly his head bobbed up inside the shadow of the cave, and they saw that he was treading water while he filled his lungs. But even as he did so, the current was carrying him farther back into the tunnel. He began to swim desperately, aiming for the lower bank of the river, but his body was chilled to the bone and his strength spent, and he made little headway.

Colum ran the length of the crag until he was beyond the point where it swallowed the river. There, he leapt down over the remnant of broken bawn, and ran across to the shore opposite Christie. Without taking time to slip out of his clothes, he anchored himself by grasping the low-hanging branch of a tree, and waded in chest-deep. Leaning out to meet the struggling swimmer, he used his free hand to grab him by the wrist and draw him in beyond the pull of the current.

A moment later, Kevin was lying, gasping and exhausted, on the grassy edge of the pasture. Christie ran back to pick up his clothes, and then followed Colum's path over the ruined bawn.

When she reached her brother's side, he gasped, "I found it, Chris, but it got away from me. The current—" He paused, sucking in air again, and said, "I tried to follow it, but the tunnel—closes down—to the top of the water."

He tried to say more, but his body began to shake violently, and his teeth chattered.

Christie snatched off her knitted beret and knelt beside him. "You almost drowned," she said, as she rubbed his wet back vigorously with the thick, warm wool. "If it hadn't been for Colum—" Her voice broke and her eyes filled with tears.

Colum stood by, shivering, while his soaked clothes dripped onto the grass.

"Don't be crying, now," he said awkwardly. "He'd have made it himself, surely. It was only by hanging onto the tree I could help him, for not one stroke can I swim."

Christie looked up at him gratefully, and it was then that she saw two men coming across the pasture toward them. They seemed to have appeared out of nowhere, and she thought of the story Mrs. O'Flaherty had told them in the night about her ancestor, Liam O'Farrell, and the men who had carried him away.

"Like any strangers," she said they had looked. But they had not been ordinary strangers.

"Kevin," Christie whispered nervously, "there are two men coming. Can you make it to get into your clothes?"

"Sure," he said, but he swayed as he tried to rise to his feet. Colum supported him quickly as Kevin took his pants from Christie and stepped into them.

"Could be it's the farmers," Colum whispered apprehensively.

"Maybe not," Christie said.

"Who then?" Colum asked.

"I was thinking of the men who carried off Liam O'Farrell and Morogh O'Lee."

"The fairies!" Colum stared at the men with shock and fear. "It could be them," he whispered, "and a mist coming down on us all of a sudden."

The fairy mist! Christie thought. In their concern over Kevin, they had not been aware of it, but it was true: the sky had darkened and a light drizzle was falling.

She remembered Mrs. O'Flaherty's warning about the locket. "Keep it on day and night," she had said.

That was impossible now: the locket was gone forever. It couldn't protect them. But the old lady had said something else. Christie found herself saying it aloud. "Pray to the saint of the ashes!"

Colum was helping Kevin into his shirt, but she saw his lips move silently as the men approached, their dark shapes somewhat obscured now by the misty rain.

"For gosh sake, Chris," said Kevin, pulling on his sweater, "you're getting as wacky as old Mrs. O'Flaherty. Those men are not supernatural, they're *farmers*, but we could be in plenty of trouble with them. It could have been their gate we broke through."

He stepped hurriedly into his loafers and stuck his socks in his pocket.

"If it's fairies from I-Brasil they are," said Colum nervously, "it's destroyed we'll be surely."

"Come on, let's make a run for it," said Kevin.

He grabbed Christie's hand and started running across the pasture, with Colum keeping pace with them, while Ben flapped out of a nearby tree and led the way. Behind them they heard the men's voices calling, but they sprinted desperately through the rain, not daring to look back to see if they were being followed.

Ahead of them, Mrs. MacAlistaire appeared on the bridge to the castle and stood waiting.

8

A Perilous Decision

Less than half an hour later they were on the fringe of the nearby town of Oughterard, and safe— or so it seemed. The rain had stopped almost as suddenly as it had begun, but there was nothing mysterious about that, for the Irish climate was completely unpredictable. Even Colum had to admit that there could be rain one moment and sun the next, and double rainbows in between.

But Christie sensed that he was as unconvinced as she about this particular rain. Had it been a fairy mist put down by the two strangers, and had they decided, when Mrs. MacAlistaire appeared on the bridge, that this was not a proper time for kidnapping?

She would never know, and she didn't want to discuss it with her mother. Mrs. MacAlistaire had been very distressed when they had told her about Kevin's icy plunge into the river, and she had given them strict orders to take no more risks of any kind. No locket on earth, and no treasure, she had insisted, was worth anything, compared to their safety. They hadn't told her why the locket had seemed so important, because it had been no time to alarm her further with old Sorcha's prophecy of impending danger. They had confined their account of the experience in the castle to the encounter with the mare and her foal, and Christie's hearing of what she thought was the ghost of a sobbing woman.

Now, they were all warm and dry. Colum had put on a set of Kevin's clothes from the extra suitcase in the trunk, and the car heater had done the rest. Mrs. MacAlistaire was driving toward the mountains and coastline of Connemara, which had once been the kingdom of the O'Flahertys. Across miles of maroon-colored bogland, they saw a massive outline of peaks against the sky.

"Twelve there are," said Colum, "the Twelve Bens, named for the giant, Ben Bola. From him I got Ben's name. A great Firbolg chieftain he was, and it's beneath those mountains he lies in his grave."

Ben, the crow, waddled across the back of the front seat, cocking his head with interest at the repeated mention of his name.

"The Firbolgs were perhaps the first colonizers of Ireland, many centuries before the birth of Christ," said Mrs. MacAlistaire. "That will give you an idea of how far back the legend of Colum's giant goes. And it's much the same with the folklore: stories of fairies are memories of earlier races, told down through the centuries, and the sites of fairy 'palaces' are often the same as the locations of ancient bronze-age dwellings."

"Mrs. O'Flaherty said that fairies are fallen angels, or maybe the dead returned," Christie declared.

"There are many explanations for the folk belief of Ireland," her mother went on, "but they can't be said to account for all the phenomena that have been documented. Some of it is still very mysterious and intriguing."

"There's one thing that intrigues me," said Kevin suddenly, "and that's the ghost Colum *thinks* Padraic saw at Aughnanure Castle."

"It's not sure I am what ghost he saw," said Colum, "but a ghost he *might* have seen, that I am sure of, because of the terrible thing that happened."

"Is this another legend?" Kevin asked challengingly.

"Legend it is not, but a true thing to be making the ghost of some woman weep."

"You mean like the one I heard?" asked Christie.

"I do," said Colum.

"When did it happen?" Kevin asked.

"In the time of the Spanish shipwrecks," said Colum.

"You mean the same time as when your great-grandmother's ancestor saved some of the sailors, and died for it?" Christie asked.

"I do," said Colum. "A cruel man there was here, made governor by the invaders, and he ordered the murder of the Spanish sailors."

Kevin was appalled. "You mean helpless men who

tried to swim ashore?"

"The same. Thousands there were, and nearly all of them murdered, for by the saving of even a few an Irishman was called a traitor, and he himself killed."

"And the O'Flahertys tried to save some?" asked Christie.

"They did," said Colum. "Murrough O'Flaherty it was, who was then Chief of the Name. Twenty he managed to save, but for that Aughnanure was captured, and his own son taken hostage."

"What happened then?" asked Kevin.

"Other Irish chiefs joined with O'Flaherty to break into Aughnanure, and that they did."

"Did they save his son?" Christie asked hopefully.

"No, they could not," said Colum bitterly. "Hanged he was, by the order of that evil man."

Suddenly Christie remembered the feeling she'd had in the castle of pressure on her throat, a feeling almost of suffocation.

"It's him I'm thinking Padraic sees, and maybe with the rope still around his neck," said Colum. "Enough it would be to put a man out of his mind entirely."

"Then the woman I heard sobbing could have been someone who loved him," said Christie.

"It could indeed," said Colum, "though many a woman there was who lived in that castle as had a grief to make her weep."

"What you heard wasn't sobbing," said Kevin decisively. "It was the wind moaning through the gun slits and loopholes."

"You don't know what I heard, any more than you know what Padraic saw," said Christie positively. "Remember what Mommy told us last summer about the house in the haunted cove: that a lot of people had been studying about hauntings for many years, and they'd discovered that even when several people were in a haunted place together, they didn't *all* see or hear the same thing."

"Yeah," Kevin admitted grudgingly, "but this was different. Anybody could tell it was the wind. Colum heard it, too."

"I wouldn't be saying what it was I heard," Colum protested, "nor what it was Christie heard, either."

"And it wasn't just the sobbing," said Christie. "It was the awful feeling I had from the minute we went inside the castle, as if the stone walls remembered all that had happened there, and I was getting their message."

"It may seem fantastic to you, Kevin," said Mrs. MacAlistaire, "but there are educated people whose research has led them to believe that inanimate matter—places, buildings, yes, even stones—do have a sort of memory which a person in a receptive state of mind may sense."

"Chris is receptive, all right," Kevin conceded, with a teasing edge in his voice.

"Yes, she is," his mother agreed. "And she would be unusually sensitive to the atmosphere, or what some people would call the "psychic ether,' of a place —especially a building like an old castle, where very crucial events may have taken place."

"I suppose it's like what you said about the old house in the cove," Kevin admitted, "that it could be 'charged' with the terrible happenings of the past, like with electricity, and Chris 'tuned in.' "

"Exactly," said his mother. "You know what *pre-cognition* is."

"It means knowing what's going to happen in the future—"

"Isn't that like old Sorcha's knowing that I'm going to find a treasure?" Christie cut in.

"*Before* you find it, yes," said Mrs. MacAlistaire. "But your feeling inside the castle, and your hearing of weeping—*if* that's what you really heard—"

"And we don't know that!" said Kevin firmly.

"No, we don't," his mother said. "But if Christie did hear and feel something that happened in the past, that's called *retrocognition*."

"Knowing what happened in the past," said Kevin, taking it in.

"Right," his mother said. "And there are authentic case histories of sensitive people who did more than hear or feel the past: they actually *saw* it, in a way that made it seem alive, as if it were happening right then."

"Holy Moses, Mom, that's crazy!" Kevin exploded.

"It's very strange indeed," his mother said, "and it all goes to prove that there's a great deal we don't know yet about the world we live in."

"I'm sure glad I'm not 'sensitive,'" said Kevin. "I don't want to feel or hear or see anything in the past —especially in old Irish castles. I'd rather see those three Irish boys out there, and what they're doing, and know it's happening *right now*!"

"Do you *know* what they're doing?" his mother asked, with a smile.

"Looks as if one of them is cutting the earth into little squares," said Kevin, "and the other two are picking it up and stacking it like a pile of bricks."

"So they are," said Colum. "Turf it is, cut out of the peat bog to dry and be burned in the fire."

"You mean that's the same stuff that Padraic burns in his fireplace?" asked Kevin.

"Him and most every other Irishman besides," said Colum.

The highway cut across miles of bogland, where the thick tussocks of moor grass and sedge were separated here and there by little ponds of water and running streamlets. Scattered clumps of gorse brightened the land with their masses of orange-colored blossoms, and the ditches along the road were lined with ferns.

Mrs. MacAlistaire slowed to a stop behind a two-wheeled cart, where a little gray donkey patiently waited his turn to pull the load of turf home. Sheep were grazing around the fringes of the bog, and where the boys were cutting into it, the color of the peat was dark red.

Christie was puzzled. "How can earth burn?" she asked.

"There's little of earth in it," said Colum. "Mostly, it's a great thickness of plants: mosses and grasses and sedge and heather."

"What soil there is has some sort of mineral in it," said Mrs. MacAlistaire, "and it's so cold and waterlogged that the grasses never disintegrate, but just pile up, layer upon layer, through the ages, until the plants become a deep interweaving of roots. If you were to walk on it, it would feel like a springy mat."

"Could we walk on it now, Mom?" Kevin asked.

"I think you've had enough of being ice cold and wet for now," his mother said. "Let's postpone that for another time."

"But not at night," Colum said.

His green-gold eyes were inscrutable, and Kevin

asked, "Why not?"

"A fearful thing there is, sometimes, in the bog after dark."

"What is it?" Christie asked, suspecting that it was something weird.

"The *solas sidh*," said Colum, his voice hushed.

"You know we don't understand Gaelic," said Kevin impatiently. "Tell us in English."

"No," said Colum, his glance resting on Christie. "This is not a time to speak of it."

"You're afraid of scaring Chris," said Kevin. "What is it? A legend about something that happened centuries ago?"

"No," said Colum sharply. "A thing that happens *now*. A thing that walks in the bog in the black of night—maybe *this* night. And if you should be there, and it come up behind you—" He broke off abruptly. "No," he said, "of this I will not speak."

Christie was thinking back to something Padraic had said about antiquities: that he could tell stories about their being found in "gardens and *peat bogs*." She hadn't known then what a peat bog was. Now it seemed to fit in with the old Gypsy's prophecy: a place where a treasure might be found, along with something else—something so frightening that Colum refused even to talk about it. Instinctively, she fumbled for the locket with its sacred ashes, and then remembered that she no longer had it to protect her.

"We're going to forget about all these eerie manifestations," her mother was saying cheerfully, "and concentrate on seeing this beautiful country of Connemara that was once ruled by the O'Flahertys."

"Did they have another castle in Connemara?"

Kevin asked.

"They did," said Colum, "and an old ruin it is, such as might well have a treasure hidden somewhere inside it."

They swung around the eastern flank of the Twelve Bens, seeing at close range the mountains that rose like pyramids from the lakes at their feet to the wind-blown sky. Driving westward over rolling green land hedged with wild fuchsias and tall rhododendron in bright shades of pink, rose and magenta, they reached the deep blue Atlantic, and were excited to realize that they were six-thousand miles away from the shores of the Pacific, where they'd spent their vacation last summer.

They followed long miles of coastline through scattered villages and along inlets where the sea turned a tropical green, and they stopped to run on white sandy beaches and discovered that for all its tempting color, the water was arctic-cold.

They passed lonely ports on land-locked harbors and saw misty islands rising out of the ocean. They rolled up hills and down across rock-strewn meadows and bogland, all of them covered with grass or moss or heather, and serving as pasture for cattle and sheep and donkeys. There were animals scattered everywhere, but most exciting were the half-wild Connemara ponies. Some were bay or brown, some were cream or gray or black, and they ran free on the green-topped cliffs with their spring foals scampering after them.

It was late by the time the travelers had completely circled the massive Twelve Bens and the coastline and arrived at the castle of Ballynahinch. It seemed to Christie that the name had a familiar ring, but she had passed through so many villages and heard the names of so many bays and inlets and islands that she couldn't place it.

Besides, this was not the original stronghold of the O'Flahertys, though it was somewhere nearby. This castle had been built later and now it was a hotel, and most important, a place where they could have dinner, for the long tour of Connemara had given them all enormous appetites.

An hour later, their hunger satisfied by a hearty Irish meal, Kevin, Christie and Colum were running along a woodland path bordered on one side by a thick stand of beech and conifer, and on the other by a rushing salmon river. Mrs. MacAlistaire had chosen to linger over after-dinner coffee in the library of the hotel, and Colum had left Ben in the car. It would not be safe to have him flying free in a strange forest with the fall of evening near.

Christie kept pace with the boys as they raced against time, for they had promised Mrs. Mac-Alistaire to be back at the hotel before dark; yet they couldn't bear to leave without seeing the ruined castle of the O'Flahertys. Farther up the sloping path, they would reach the source of the river, Ballynahinch Lake. A bridge marked the point where the lake narrowed to spill itself down in foaming cataracts, and from there they would be able to see the old fortress.

The sky seemed to be darkening prematurely, and they saw that a thickening mass of clouds was creeping down over the nearby peaks of the Bens, bringing with it a rush of icy air that pierced the thick wool of their caps and sweaters.

Christie stopped running to catch her breath and

stared skyward in concern. "Is it going to storm?" she asked.

"No," said Colum, pausing beside her. "A trick of the Bens it is, to be drawing the clouds down around them like cloaks to keep their sleeping giant warm throughout the night."

A final spurt of running brought them to the bridge. Far out in the lake, on an island nearer to the opposite shore than to them, they spotted the castle. Distance and the gray overcast made it impossible to see more than the square outline of a tower.

"I wish we could get closer," Kevin said. "I wonder if there's a path around the lake."

"A path *across* it we need," said Colum excitedly, "and the means is right before us, if you're looking at what I'm seeing!"

Following his eyes, they saw a rowboat moored to a small landing beyond the bridge.

"And with the oars boated," said Kevin, catching Colum's enthusiasm. "Why not? We can make it over and back before dark."

"The boat must be for the use of the hotel guests," said Christie doubtfully.

"Didn't I just eat the grandest meal of my life there?" Colum asked. "It's guests we are, the four of us."

"We're guests enough for a quick ride when nobody's using the boat," Kevin declared. "Come on, Chris, we haven't got time to argue."

"And it's there your treasure could be waiting," Colum said persuasively.

Kevin was already running to the landing, and moments later they had cast off, with Christie in the bow, Colum in the stern, and Kevin at the oars. The lowering clouds were a steel gray now, and a chill breeze sprang up, riffling the water so that it slapped hard against the sides of the boat, but Kevin pulled strongly toward the island.

They could see it more clearly as they moved out into the lake, and everything on it seemed green, for not only was the earth covered with shrubs and grasses, but the stone walls of the castle were completely blanketed with green-leafed vines. The buildings were more extensive than they had judged from the shore, and they felt a thrill of anticipation—and of apprehension—at the thought of exploring them.

Christie's thoughts returned to the name Ballynahinch, and suddenly her mind made the connection: Morogh O'Lee! Padraic himself had said it: that the kidnapping of Morogh O'Lee had taken place on the shore of Ballynahinch, *which used to be O'Flaherty land.*

Shocked at the realization, she said aloud, "This is the place!"

"What place?" Kevin demanded, gasping from the exertion of rowing.

"The place where the fairies kidnapped Morogh O'Lee. Padraic told us this morning that Morogh was walking along the shore of Ballynahinch when the fairies blindfolded him and carried him off. We're in the exact place!"

"No," said Colum, "the shore of the loch it was not, but the shore of the sea, where the river goes down to meet it."

But even in the gray of the overcast, she saw that his face had paled. "What difference does it make?" she demanded. "Ballynahinch is still the place where the fairies were."

Kevin didn't answer her. The wind had stiffened suddenly, whipping the lake into angry little waves, and the work of rowing against them was becoming too heavy for him to manage alone.

"Better give me a hand," he told Colum. "You take one oar, I'll keep the other, and we'll pull together. And don't stand up!" he commanded sharply as Colum started to rise from his seat in the stern. "You'll capsize us. Crawl over."

When Colum had taken his place beside Kevin, they began to row. At first, they couldn't pull in unison, and the little boat twisted from side to side alarmingly, but gradually, with Kevin shouting "Now!" at each dip of the oars, the rhythm of their stroking improved.

The lake had looked small and the distance to the island short when they started, but the longer they rowed the farther away it seemed. The water became increasingly choppy, and crouching in the bow, Christie warned, "We'd better turn back, Kevin!"

He glanced over his shoulder. "We're closer to the island," he said. "We'd better settle for that. The wind'll go down later on."

"Not before dark," Christie said. It felt as if it were blowing straight off the glaciers of the north Atlantic, she thought, and the waves, chopping and breaking, were spraying ice-water into their faces. The boys strained on the oars, putting their full strength behind each stroke, but they seemed to be making no headway. The force of the gale was blowing them off their course, and they saw that it was no longer possible to aim for the island.

The shore of the lake, as far around as they could see, was studded with thick woods, and the light was dwindling. The waves, slapping higher, were surging over the rails of the little craft, threatening to swamp her, and Christie crawled back to the stern. Taking off her loafers, she began to bail with them, but though she scooped out the water till her arms were stiff with pain, she might as well have been using a teacup.

"A desperate night it is," said Colum, shivering with cold and fear, "and it's lucky we'll be if we're not destroyed in it."

"If we can keep her bow into the wind we'll ride it out," said Kevin, "but if the wind turns her head and the waves hit us broadside, we'll go over. So keep rowing, guy, keep rowing!"

The two boys rowed frantically, desperately, though their shoulders ached and their legs were cramped, and Christie knelt in the stern, dizzy and half-sick, but continuing to bail out what water she could. All of them realized that the best they could hope for was to keep afloat until they reached some shore.

But the solid earth with its shadowy mass of forest faded into darkness before they could reach it. Only by the feel of the wind on his back could Kevin guess whether they were keeping the boat headed into it or not.

Though their oars felt as if they were weighted with lead, the boys kept stroking furiously, but at length Kevin knew they were losing their fight, and that the wind had turned her head, for the little craft began to pitch and roll helplessly, and no matter how savagely they struggled, they couldn't turn her back again.

Hearts pounding with terror, the three of them kept up the useless fight, while the boat wallowed and they knew that at any minute they might be pitched headlong into the black swirling waters. A sudden wild gust sent a high wave battering against the craft broadside, and as she rolled, her rail grazed against stone. Rolling with her, Kevin felt his oar strike land. Reaching out with his hand, he touched the branches of a bush.

"We're safe!" he shouted. "We've made it!"

Hardly daring to believe in the miracle of their escape, they clambered cautiously out of the tossing boat. Finding the earth real and solid beneath their feet, they collapsed onto the grassy little point of land and lay limp and silent, breathing prayers of thankfulness.

When the boys had gathered enough strength, they pulled the little boat up onto the shore and tied her bowline to a tree. Around them, the night was black as jet, and they had no clue to where they were or which way they should head.

9

Footprints of Fire

There was no time to wait for the black shroud of clouds to open and let a glimpse of moon or starlight shine through to guide them. Colum knew the clouds were more likely to thicken until they were split by lightning and thunder and rain poured down.

Water and shore and forest were almost indivisible in the blackness. If there was any light at the boat landing on the opposite side of the lake, it was hidden from view by one of the points of land that reached out like fingers from the shore, or by a small island. And the castle-hotel was invisible, too, its lights cut off, probably, by some rise of land or by the thickness of the woods.

Kevin and Christie knew their mother would be frantic with worry, and they had to find their way back to her as quickly as possible. But how? They were lost in a black wilderness, with no choice but to fumble their way into the forest.

They moved cautiously, their hands outstretched before them to prevent a head-on collision with the trees which, in their thick mass, had no shape. The ground underfoot was rough and uneven, and though they took one careful step at a time, they stumbled over rocks and groped through thickets.

At first they tried to follow each other, with the boys leading the way to protect Christie, but when they came upon no path, they fanned out separately, hoping to triple their chances. They kept in close touch by voice, and at intervals they stopped to shout, knowing that by now Mrs. MacAlistaire would have searchers out looking for them, but either they were too far away or their voices were lost on the wind, for they heard no response.

Pushing ahead on her own, Christie fumbled through a dark mass of breast-high growth, pressing it apart to make her way, and suddenly her hands and the side of her face where she'd leaned into it were stinging as if she'd touched a thousand hot needles. She gasped with shock at the sharp pain of it, but said nothing.

Time stretched out agonizingly, while the wind moaned through the trees and every branch and tangle of bushes seemed to reach out like an unseen enemy to grasp them.

It was too dangerous to continue to fan out in three directions lest they become separated, so they came together and plodded on, groping through woods and tangled thickets, scrambling up hill and plunging down again, until at last they came upon a pathway. None of them knew whether to follow it to the right or left. Colum made the choice, and they let him lead them, grateful for smoother ground beneath their feet and the narrow opening through the black forest.

But after a period of patient tracking, the ground underfoot changed abruptly, and they were no longer walking on firm earth, but on something moist and springy, like a thick layer of soggy hay. Though the night was still pitch black, somehow they sensed that they had emerged from the woods into a sort of clearing, and when Kevin and Christie reached out their arms, they touched no branches or bushes.

In a flash, Kevin remembered what his mother had said: "If you were to walk on it, it would feel like a springy mat."

The bog! he thought, and remembered also what Colum had said about the fearful thing that walked there in the night. He hoped Christie wouldn't realize where they were, but in the same instant she whispered, "Kevin, we're on the bog!"

Colum was a few steps ahead of them, and as he turned back they all saw the terrifying footprints. They stretched between him and them, and they were outlined in green fire.

"The *solas sidh*!" Colum gasped in horror.

"What is it?" Kevin whispered, awed in spite of himself.

"The fairy fire. A warning it is to get off the bog. It's back we must go."

"Back where?"

"Back to the woods."

"Not on your life!" Kevin declared.

But Christie had turned toward the forest. "Look!" she whispered in dismay.

Behind them the footprints stretched back in two chains of fire that glowed with an unearthly ice green.

"They're behind us, not ahead of us," said Kevin, looking beyond Colum.

"They're all around us," said Christie fearfully, for at a distance on both sides of them she saw other prints, not the same shape, but in chains of the same green fire.

"It's following us they are," said Colum, "warning us to get off the bog or we'll never be seen again by mortal eyes."

"You mean we'll be carried off like Morogh O'Lee?" Christie asked.

"Carried off, buried in our graves, who knows what?" said Colum. "It's disappear we will, like many another before us, if we don't get ourselves off in time."

"Rubbish!" said Kevin. "We can't go back into the woods. We'd be stuck there all night. Besides, how do we know your 'fairies' aren't hiding there in the dark? We don't know what's in that forest, but we do know we've got to get back to that hotel."

"It's miles of bog there could be ahead of us," said Colum, the shrillness of panic in his voice.

"There are miles of forest and lake behind us," said Kevin firmly, "and I don't want any more of that. There's better going here on the bog. Come on, I'll lead."

He reached out in the dark to take Christie's hand, but she drew back at the brush of his fingers.

"Don't touch my hands," she cried, "they're on fire."

"What do you mean?" Kevin demanded.

"I don't know," she said. "It was a bush I pushed through in the woods, and suddenly I felt as if I'd touched a thousand burning needles. It's on my face, too."

"Wow!" said Kevin. "It must be stinging nettles. Come on then, follow me."

He moved forward boldly in the darkness, and with each step he left a fiery footprint. Christie followed the eerie green tracks and heard Colum, behind her, groaning, "It's taken we will be, surely."

Kevin turned back and seeing the weird imprints, felt an alarm he wouldn't admit, even to himself.

"Let's run," he said, and then quickly covering with an excuse, he added, "it's colder out here in the open."

They were already chilled to the bone by the night air and the wind, but the horror of the unearthly green footprints following them step for step turned their blood to ice. Kevin was leaping from tussock to tussock, and Christie and Colum stumbled after him, led by the glowing green fire.

Soon they were all racing in a wild panic, sliding, skidding, falling on the moist turf, and staggering up to run again. When they had to stop, gasping to get their breath, they looked back and saw three green chains of fire pursuing them, as if there were three invisible demons right at their heels. And still at a distance, but closing in now, were the other green imprints of their diabolical assistants.

In a frenzy of terror, Colum shot ahead of Kevin

and Christie, running, he was sure, for his very life, and they found themselves tearing after him, their hearts pounding till they could barely breathe. The outer circle of fire that had been closing in broke open at their approach, and they rushed through it, stumbling down into a ditch and up the other side to find themselves on a hard dirt road.

Before they had time to debate which way to go, a car swung onto the road and they ran, shouting with relief, toward its headlights. It was a little pickup truck, and the driver was Fergal McFirbis, the gardener of the Ballynahinch estate. From him they learned that he was but one of many searchers, some of them scouring the woods and hills on foot and bicycle, but only he knew that the rowboat was missing.

" 'Twas I meself as tied the boat up there," he said, "and I was not after telling your mother, and having her go half out of her head with the worry of it. And we'll not be speaking of it now, atall, atall," he added. " 'Twas I as found it, where you'd tied it to the tree, and claimed it was I meself as had done it. And when you were nowhere to be seen in the woods, I thought of the bog, and got into me truck and came round by this old back road."

It was then Colum told him of the fairy fire.

"Makes a body's blood run cold to think of it," said Fergal, with a shiver. "A blessing it is you got away and out of it at the double quick, and I here in time to meet you."

As he swung the truck away from the bog and onto the main road, Kevin saw that there had been sheep grazing around them in a wide circle. It must have

been their hoofprints, he thought, that had made the smaller tracks of green fire.

When they were approaching the hotel, Fergal slowed down as he crossed the bridge to remind them once more: " 'Tis a secret between us about the boat," he said, "for no one there was who could have gone out on the lake in such a wind to hunt for you, and 'twould be giving your mother a sickness to be thinking about the danger of it, even now."

"We'll tell her some other time, when it's long past," said Kevin. "By then she'll know we wouldn't chance it again."

"I'd be for not telling atall, atall," said Fergal, "but for now we'll be saying it was lost in the woods you were, by taking the wrong turn on the trail—for that's what you did, indeed, when you left the boat."

"We'll want to tell her about the bog and the fairy fire," Christie said.

"That you can," said Fergal, "for she won't be knowing that it's only by the blessing of God and Mary that you came out of it atall."

When they reached the castle-hotel and ran into their mother's waiting arms, Kevin and Christie knew Fergal McFirbis had been right: Mrs. MacAlistaire was the kind of woman who was outwardly calm in any crisis, but the tears of relief in her eyes and the paleness of her face betrayed the strain she'd been under. It was fortunate that she hadn't known they'd been out on the lake and nearly drowned.

Sitting before a glowing turf in the library, they'd been thoroughly warmed with hot milk and sandwiches, and they'd spoken of the fairy fire. One of

the guests, an Englishman who came to Ballynahinch every spring to fish in the lakes and river, said
the green fire was some kind of phosphorescence such
as he'd seen in tropical seas. It happened in the bog
only when climatic conditions were right, usually in
winter, and he admitted that this night was as cold
as any in January.

His explanation impressed Kevin, but not the Irish
guests. They didn't care to argue the point for fear
they'd be ridiculed, but the Englishman had to con-
fess that he'd never seen the fairy fire himself. To
those who knew the bogs of Connemara and what had
happened there, Christie and Kevin and Colum had
been very lucky indeed to escape with their lives. The
fairy fire, in their opinion, was a supernatural and
dangerous phenomenon. Christie found it hard to
doubt them.

There was no way to reach the O'Flahertys, for
they had no phone, so late as it was, they set out on
the long drive back to the farm. The boys fell asleep
almost instantly in the back seat, with Ben huddled
on Colum's shoulder. Christie sat in front with her
mother, but she couldn't keep her eyes open. Her
blistered hands and cheek had been eased by a soothing lotion, and soon exhaustion overcame her and she,
too, drifted off. Mrs. MacAlistaire drove the long,
lonely miles east to the city of Galway, and then
swung south toward the farm.

10

The Well of the Seven Daughters

It was early morning when Christie was awakened
by the burning irritation of her hands and face. For
a moment she was surprised to find herself in the
snug little bed of the O'Flaherty loft. She'd been so
sound asleep she barely remembered their arrival
there the night before. Hardly more than half con-
scious, she and Kevin had managed to get into their
pajamas and slip into beds warmed by hot-water
bottles; then they had floated off again into a deep
slumber.

Now, in the room below, she heard the soft murmur
of voices and smelled the delicious fragrance of bread
baking. She looked at her hands. The swelling had
gone down, but they were covered with a stinging
red rash, and her cheek had the same itching, burning sensation. Perhaps if she could dip them into

cool water, she thought, the irritation might be eased.

She slipped into her bathrobe and peered down over the edge of the loft. Padraic was having tea with his mother. He caught sight of Christie at once, and with a bright smile of welcome, motioned for her to come down. She climbed down the stair-ladder and they all whispered so as not to wake her mother.

It was Mrs. O'Flaherty who noticed her hands before she could speak of the annoying rash. "It's to the holy well you must go," she whispered earnestly. "The well of the Seven Daughters. Not far from here it is, near the ruined church and the tower. Dip your poor little hands, and your face, too, in the sacred waters, and it's healed they'll be, entirely."

She drew back the curtain at the window and looked up at the gray mass of clouds that spanned the sky as far as the eye could see. "It's now you must go," she added, "for it's likely they'll be opening to pour down their rain on us, later in the day. Colum can take you, for there's no work he has to do but begging and stealing," she added, with a twinkle in her eyes, "and it's better off he'll be, driving you to the holy well in the two-wheeled cart."

"It is, indeed," Padraic said, with a grin, "and I'll be going down now to the camp and getting him up while you wake your brother."

He went out the door, closing it softly after him, and Mrs. O'Flaherty went to her pot oven, hanging over the turf fire.

"It's ready for you, when you're dressed," she said, lifting the lid and letting the wonderful smell of the bread fill the room. "A hot breakfast I'll have for you, and then you can go quickly to heal your hands, and I'll be the one to tell your mother when she wakes. That way she won't be worrying."

And so it was that in less than half an hour, Christie and Kevin were starting off with Colum in a two-wheeled Gypsy cart drawn by a lively brown Connemara pony, while Ben flew overhead, expressing his pleasure in loud caws and shrieks.

The cart was padded with a thick bed of straw, but surprisingly Colum had brought along not only spades and flashlights, but a short ladder.

"What's all this stuff for?" Kevin asked.

"You'll be finding out," said Colum mysteriously, "for by going into the nettles, it's Christie herself may have been leading us to the very place where the treasure is hidden."

"You mean the holy well?" she asked.

"Not the well itself, but a place near it."

"The ruined church then, and the tower?"

"No ordinary church and tower it is," said Colum, "but I'll not be speaking of it till Christie is there to see for herself."

"You think she's going to see something nobody else will see," said Kevin astutely.

"I'll not be saying 'yes' or 'no,'" said Colum, and his eyes had that unreadable look they'd seen before, but Kevin and Christie guessed that the answer was "yes." The thought of old ruins and ghosts made Christie shiver, and she wished that she were still wearing the locket with its sacred ashes.

They were approaching a small village now, where the houses were closer together. To Kevin's and Christie's surprise, they saw Colum's pretty red-haired mother going up to the door of the first house, and she was carrying in her arms her youngest child.

Colum drove by as if he hadn't recognized her, and farther up the road on the opposite side, they saw Colum's grandmother, Kate, the wife of Seamus, the fiddler. She, too, was walking up the path to a house, while Colum's younger brothers and sisters tagged after her. They pretended not to see Colum as the cart rolled past them.

Suddenly Christie remembered what old Mrs. O'Flaherty had said about begging and stealing.

"Why didn't you speak to your family?" she asked.

"It's begging they are," he said matter-of-factly, "and how would it look to the women in the houses for me to be driving by with a fine Connemara pony, and two rich American friends in their grand Aran sweaters and caps? And in the same minute, my mother and grandmother are saying the children are starving, and could they maybe have a loaf of bread, or an egg for the youngest, or a potato or two?"

"Why do they beg?" Kevin asked.

"How else would we live?" Colum countered.

"By working," said Kevin. "Your father and grandfather are working now, for Padraic."

"It's little enough work there is for anybody, and even less for a tinker. And few are the men who will hire them. Beggars and thieves they say we are."

"You mean you steal, too?" Kevin asked in astonishment.

"We do," said Colum candidly. "A chicken, maybe, or milk from a cow, or eggs from a hen house." He grinned roguishly. "Or anything that's laid out, begging to be taken. But criminals we are not," he said, his voice suddenly defensive and proud. "It's not tinkers who do the big robbing and the killing. Travelers we are, begging and stealing only enough to keep us alive."

"And they give you food, even if they don't like you?" asked Kevin.

"They do," said Colum, "for it's their Christian duty, they're thinking, to keep us from starving. And some there are who are friends to us, like Padraic and his mother, and let us stay on their land and give the men a bit of work to be doing."

"Haven't you ever lived in a house?" Christie asked.

"I have not," said Colum. "Born under a wagon I was, and my father before me. People of the roads we are, and a good life it is, surely. But if I had me a bit of money—" He paused and that same roguish grin lit his face. "Or if it was me was to find a treasure, it's sell it I would for a bag of gold, and go by myself to roam the roads of the world." He sighed regretfully. "But it's you as will find it, Christie," he said, "for what my great-grandmother saw in the cards is what will be coming true."

The well proved to be much farther away than Mrs. O'Flaherty had remembered, and even Ben was glad to rest from his flying by riding on the rump of his friend, the Connemara pony. The clouds had turned to a deep blue and black, and there was an ominous rumble of thunder when at last Colum spotted the round tower.

"It's almost there we are," he said, "and when you've put your hands in the holy well, it's the tower will give us shelter."

"Who were the Seven Daughters of the well?" Christie asked.

"It's saints they were," said Colum, "or some say they were the daughters of an Irish king, back in the time of the legends, but whichever they were, it's healed you will be by the waters of their well."

He pulled up before the roofless ruins of a church, built where centuries earlier a monastery had stood. It had a mournful and deserted look, for weeds and grasses and bracken had taken over the sacred grounds, growing in wild profusion in the church-yard and even inside the melancholy gray stone walls. But someone had made a narrow path that cut through the rank green growth, and following it, they came upon the holy well.

It lay in the hollow of a rock, like an oval basin filled with water that was crystal clear. A stone wall had been built in a semi-circle two-thirds of the distance around it, and over the wall hung a tangle of wild red roses. Christie knelt on the pale stone in front of it, and felt her knees fit into hollows that had been worn, perhaps, by kneeling pilgrims over the centuries.

The boys stood behind her, and she forgot their presence as she dipped her red and burning hands into the pure cold water. To her surprise, she felt a gentle movement, and searching the depths of the basin, she saw tiny ripples of light at one end where the water flowed up from some hidden spring within the rock itself and then at the opposite end, disappeared, as though the stone were porous, for the level of the well was unchanging.

She didn't know who the Seven Daughters were—

whether they were indeed saints, or legendary
princesses—but there was a feeling of quiet beauty
in the little shrine, a sense of something truly sacred
and long-revered. Christie closed her eyes and murmured a prayer that was both an asking and a thank-
ing for the healing of the holy well. She let her hands
linger in the gentle, soothing flow, and then, holding
back her blonde hair, she lay her cheek on the crystal
waters. The purity and coolness seemed to wash
away all the burning irritation of the rash, and
when she lifted her head and dipped both hands once
more into the well, the redness had faded, and she
felt her prayer was being answered.

She rose from her knees and turned around, only
to discover that the boys had gone. Overhead, the
clouds were black as ink, and somewhere there was
a streak of lightning and a rumble of thunder. She
ran down the path to where they had left the cart and
pony, and it was not there. She was alone in the
deserted ruins, and the thought gave her a prickly
feeling down her back. What had Colum meant when
he said that by going into the nettles she might have
been leading them to where the treasure was hidden?
Not the well, but the place near it. It was no ordinary
church and tower, he had said. *The tower!*

She ran to where she could see it looming against
the black sky, a great tower of stone, tall and round
and tapered, and several stories high. It looked almost like a moon rocket, and to her relief, the boys
were there. Colum had stopped the cart just beneath
the door, which for some strange reason was at least
ten feet above the ground. He and Kevin had placed
the ladder against the wall of the tower, but even

with the bottom of it standing in the cart, the top rung was still a good three feet short.

The first big drops of rain began to fall, and Christie ran to the cart and clambered up into it. Kevin was already climbing the ladder while Colum steadied it. The heavy wooden door with its shield of metal plating was ajar, and reaching for the threshold, Kevin got a grip on it. Then digging his toes into the tiny crevices between the stones, he pulled himself up. Once inside, he called, "Come on, Chris, and hurry. It's going to pour!"

Christie climbed the little ladder until she could grasp her brother's hand, and he pulled her up and helped her swing over into the shelter of the tower. Then climbing up the first rungs, Colum handed up the two spades and pocketed the flashlights. The Connemara pony was becoming nervous, and with no one to steady the ladder for him, Colum's position was precarious. He backed down and took a length of sturdy rope from under the straw. Tieing one end of it to his end of the reins, he flung the rest up to Kevin. Then with Kevin controlling the pony, he talked soothingly to the animal as he moved up the ladder. When he could reach the threshold he pulled himself up, and while Kevin held the pony in check, Colum pulled the ladder up after him.

They were all safely inside, and Ben had long since flown to the sill of an upper window and was cawing down at them. But there was still the pony and cart to secure. Colum tied a large knot in the rope that held the reins, and then with knot still in hand, let the rope lie across the corner of the threshold.

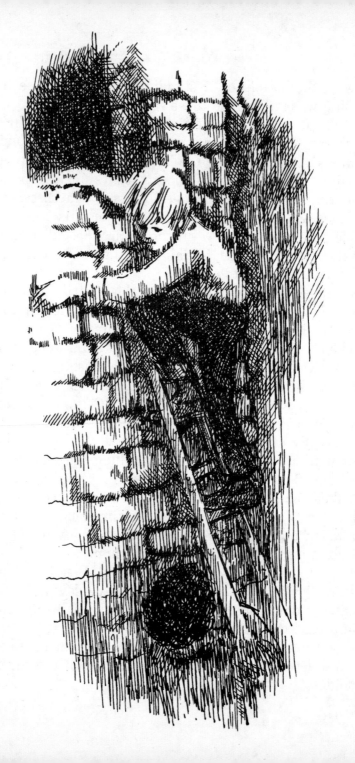

"Now!" he commanded, and Kevin pushed the heavy door onto the rope, but it was not closed tightly enough to hold against the tugging of a frightened horse. With the knot still inside, the two boys pushed together until at last the door was closed all the way. Then they put a heavy wooden bar in place across it.

Without the open door, the room seemed totally dark. Colum fumbled in his pocket for a flashlight, but before he could switch it on Christie whispered, "We're not alone. There's somebody else in this room!"

11

Sorcha's Prophecy — the Treasure

"Give me a flashlight!" Kevin whispered urgently.

"Wait!" said Colum, his voice barely audible.

They stood tense and motionless, not knowing who might be there or what menace they might be facing. Gradually, as their eyes became adjusted to the change, they realized that the room was not totally dark. A faint light was filtering down through a narrow slit of window high above them, but it didn't penetrate the shadows to reveal what might be lurking there.

"Give me a flash!" Kevin hissed commandingly.

"I will not!" Colum whispered, equally determined.

The three of them stared into the shadows, seeing only that the room was round, with a floor of heavy planking, and that a ladder led to the story above. Somewhere up there, Ben let out a squawk that sounded like a question, and when no one answered, he lapsed into silence.

"Christie," Colum whispered anxiously, "who is it that is here?"

"I don't know," she answered.

"Is it somebody you're seeing, or somebody you're feeling?"

"I didn't see—" she began.

But at that moment there was a flash of lightning and this time the roll of thunder was closer. Kevin saw at once that the room was empty, but Christie was staring at something and Colum was watching her.

"It was seeing you were, when the lightning flashed," said Colum.

"It was like white smoke," said Christie, "only it had a shape."

"It was the glare through the window," said Kevin decisively.

"It's not you that's knowing what it was," said Colum. "Had it the shape of a man, Christie?"

"It didn't have any shape," said Kevin disgustedly. "You're putting the whole thing into her head."

"Am I now? Was it me as said there was somebody with us in this room?"

"Whoever said it was *wrong*," Kevin declared. "Give me a flashlight!"

Colum pulled one out of his pants pocket, and Kevin snatched it, switched it on, and sent its beam probing around the circular room. This time they saw clearly what they had seen before, except that Kevin noticed there was a second door swung back against the wall. The stone wall itself, between the outer door which they had closed, and the inner door, was at least three feet thick.

"What kind of a place is this?" Kevin asked.

"A watch-tower it is," said Colum, "a kind of fortress built a thousand years ago."

"A thousand years!" Christie exclaimed.

"Put up, it was, to protect the monastery that lies outside there, with its ruins beneath the grasses."

"Didn't protect it very well," Kevin commented.

"Protected all of them as lived in it, for it was here they took shelter in times of attack for hundreds of years," said Colum, "until at last the invading foreigners set fire to the tower itself."

"A stone tower? How could they do that?" Kevin asked.

"Flung a flaming torch in through a window, and a floor caught fire before the unlucky monks could reach it."

"What happened to them?" Christie asked in concern.

"What could happen?" Colum countered. "Like a chimney a round tower is, with one window at each story, and four at the top—"

"Making a perfect draft," said Kevin, getting the picture. "Boy, what a deathtrap. It must have gone up like a torch!"

"Not the only tower it was, as went like a torch. Many there were that burned, trapping in them the monks and their treasures, and once even a High King."

"How awful!" said Christie, shivering with the horror of the disasters as she saw them in her imagination.

"But a strange story there is about the monks here, and the burning. It was Padraic told me."

"You say they kept treasures here?" Kevin asked.

"In all the towers, they kept their treasures high up." He nodded his head toward the top stories.

"Let's go up," Kevin said. "You go first, Colum, with Chris in the middle. I'll come up beneath her, just in case she should fall."

"But there couldn't be treasures now," Christie said. "Not after it all burned."

"No; rebuilt the inside was, maybe two hundred years ago, but we'll go up," said Colum, heading toward the ladder, "for who's to say what there may be to see?"

Kevin beamed his light onto the ladder and Colum started up.

"Solid it is, still," he said, "so it's safe, Christie."

Christie followed him up the long ladder, and when she had reached the next floor, Colum beamed his flash down, to light Kevin's climb. The second story was like the first, with the narrow window facing in a different direction, and all of it empty.

They climbed up to the third, where Ben greeted them excitedly, chattering and croaking as he planted himself on Colum's head. There was another blaze of lightning outside the window, and the thunder was louder, nearer, but the rain was still light.

Kevin noticed the stone hooks on the walls. "What were these for?" he asked.

"The hanging of the satchels for the books and bells, Padraic says, for it was on this floor and those still higher that they kept their greatest treasures: the hand-written books and the golden bells and the crozier, maybe, of the patron saint, and chalices and the like. And if there were great people like a bishop or a High King staying in the monastery, it was to the highest parts of the tower they were taken, to keep them safe from the showers of arrows shot by their enemies."

"What was the strange story about the monks here and the burning?" Kevin asked.

"It was burned they all were, and their precious relics with them, it was said, for when it was over and the coals at the bottom cooled, there was nothing to be found. Yet those same monks were seen, ten of them, alive and well, far to the north in Donegal," said Colum. "But one was missing, for eleven monks had been in the tower." He paused, as though he were not sure how much of the tale he should tell. He walked to the narrow slit of a window that over-looked the ruins of the monastery, which had been built long before the roofless church.

"Christie," he said, "would you come to be looking down with me?"

She came to the window, and Kevin followed to peer over her shoulder.

"Is there anything you're seeing now, besides the broken walls and the wild grasses?" Colum asked.

"I see the holy well," she said, and remembered to look at her hands. The rash had faded almost entirely.

"Besides the well," Colum said. "Anything like the wisp of smoke with a shape to it, walking from the tower to the monastery and beckoning for a person to be following it?"

"N-no," Christie said, "but even if it were there, I don't think I could see it in the rain."

"A *ghost*, you could see," said Colum, almost pleadingly. "Look now, again—look for the ghost of the monk!"

"You mean, the ghost of the eleventh monk has been seen walking from the tower to the monastery?" Kevin asked.

"He has," said Colum, "for Padraic himself has told me of it, but long ago. I don't know how long. Walked, the monk did, and beckoned, Padraic said, but no one would follow him, for it was afraid they were to follow the dead."

"Well, we don't have to worry," said Kevin calmly, "because he isn't down there. He probably got tired of beckoning and lay down to rest, maybe in one of those old graves that's covered with weeds."

Suddenly the sky above them seemed to be split open by a great zigzagging streak of lightning that momentarily blinded them, and an instant later, a clap of thunder shook the tower. Ben screeched in terror, and far below, they heard the pony scream with fear.

"That almost hit us," said Kevin. "Let's get out of here!"

He ran for the ladder and backed down it as rapidly as he could go, shouting for them to follow him without waiting. At the bottom, he held his flash up to guide them, as Christie came down next and Colum only a rung above her.

The clouds had burst open and the rain was pouring down in great sheets of water. Ben fluttered wildly around inside the tower and then landed on the window sill and took off, flying for the shelter of nearby trees.

"Lightning it was, struck the top once before, and split the cap off it," said Colum, as they started down the lower ladder.

"You mean the top of *this* tower was struck?" asked Kevin.

"I do," said Colum, moving down swiftly. "Did you not see the top was missing?"

"Wow!" said Kevin, skipping the last rungs to jump down to the floor. "We could be barbecued in here just like your monk and your king!"

He ran to the door and lifted away the heavy wooden bar. Colum reached the bottom and hurried to untie the knot in the rope. He had done too good a job of tightening it, and the going was slow.

Kevin was already grasping the handle. "For Pete's sake, hurry!" he commanded.

"It's hurrying I am," Colum retorted nervously, bruising his fingers in the struggle.

When finally he succeeded in loosening the knot, Kevin pulled on the door, but nothing happened. In surprise, he braced his feet against the high stone threshold and leaned back to pull again mightily, but still the door wouldn't budge.

"It's stuck!" he grunted in dismay. "Help me!"

Colum placed his hands alternately with Kevin's on the large wooden handle, and side by side, they braced their feet against the stone.

"Now *pull!*" Kevin shouted.

They pulled together, but the door didn't move an inch.

Another blaze of lightning seemed to streak down through the small window above them and the fortress shuddered with the thunderbolt that followed.

"It's still playing with this tower!" Kevin shouted over the downpour outside. "Come on, we've got to try again."

Braced, and with their strong four-handed grip, they gritted their teeth, pulling desperately. The handle gave way and they fell backwards to the floor with it loose in their hands. The door remained firmly fixed.

"Swollen by the rain it must be, and the rope, too, making it tight," said Colum dejectedly.

"We're trapped!" Kevin groaned. "There's no other way out of here. Those window slits are too narrow to squeeze through."

"Excepting those at the top," said Colum, "and it's struck by lightning we'd be there, or killed if we jumped, for it's eighty feet surely."

"*I saw him!*" Christie whispered.

"Who?" Kevin demanded.

"The monk," she said, her voice hushed with awe. "He was standing right there." She pointed to an opening where a ladder descended to the lowest level of the tower.

"You saw the lightning reflected on the stone," Kevin scoffed.

"I saw the monk," Christie declared quietly but positively.

"Chris—" Kevin began, but Colum cut in.

"Hist!" he whispered. "It's not for you to be calling her a liar, and with the ghost of a holy man here in the room."

"I wasn't," Kevin protested. "I only mean she thinks she saw his ghost because of the story you told. She's imagining—"

"He's there now!" Christie cut in, in a whisper.

"I don't see him," said Kevin, out loud. "Do you, Colum?"

"I do not," Colum whispered, "and isn't that just what my great-grandmother was saying? That *we* wouldn't be seeing whatever it was, but Christie would?"

"He's disappearing slowly down the ladder," Christie whispered.

"Beckoning he is," said Colum, in awed wonder. "It's down there he wants her to come, following after him."

"What's down there?" Kevin asked.

"Nothing but the ground itself—"

"The ground!" Kevin exclaimed. "Monk or no monk, it's an idea. Maybe we can dig out. Grab your spade and let's go!"

He picked up a spade and one of the flashlights which was lying, lighted, on the floor. Colum grabbed the other spade and flash and followed him toward the ladder. To their surprise, Christie had already started down into the darkness below.

Kevin sent the flash beaming along her line of descent to guide her, but she seemed to be moving down automatically, rung by rung, her eyes focused on something beyond his view. When she reached the bottom, she walked almost as if in a trance toward whatever it was she was seeing.

Kevin climbed down the ladder quickly, with Colum descending on the rungs just above him.

"He was standing right here and pointing down," Christie said, and her voice sounded strange and far away. "He wants us to dig in this spot."

Kevin started to protest, but he stopped himself. He'd meant to say that what she'd seen *had* to be the light from their flashes filtering down through the cracks between the planked floor above, or beamed down at a slant on the ladder, but he knew it was useless. Both Christie and Colum were convinced that what she was seeing was the ghost of the monk, and there was no point in arguing further.

"Is he gone now?" he asked.

"He vanished when you came down with your flashlights," she said, "but while it was still dark I could see him clearly. He motioned for me to follow him, and when he got here he pointed at the ground. I think he wants us to go down."

"Maybe it's there the treasure is hidden," Colum exclaimed excitedly.

"It'd be better if it was a secret passage out of here," said Kevin, not meaning it seriously. Then suddenly something clicked in his mind. "Hey!" he shouted. "That would explain it!"

"Explain what?" Christie asked.

"How the ten monks were seen alive and well in Donegal. They didn't burn. They got out of here!"

"And the eleventh—" she began.

"He didn't make it," said Kevin.

"But he knew the way," said Christie thoughtfully, "and now he's showing us!"

"We'll soon find out," said Kevin. "Come on, Colum, let's dig!" He handed his flashlight to Christie. "You beam this onto the spot while we work."

In the transfer from his hand to hers, the light illumined Colum's face for just an instant, and Christie saw that his eyes had a wild eager look as he jumped on his spade haft, driving it into the ground. Kevin, too, pressed his spade into the earth, but his intensity was directed toward escape from the fury of the storm outside, and the danger of fire in the tower. Colum, she knew, had forgotten the lightning; he was thinking only of the treasure.

The soil was not too hard, for the abundant rains of Ireland had poured down through the broken cap of the tower, dripped through the cracks between the planks of the flooring, and moistened even this most sheltered area. The boys dug fiercely, each compelled by his own purpose. Keeping pace with each other, they rhythmically jumped on the hafts of their spades, drove them deep, scooped the soil up, and threw it to one side.

When they were down two feet, they had to widen the hole so they could both stand in it as they dug.

"There's something mixed in with this soil," said Kevin. "The farther down we go, the more there is of it." He stopped digging to pick it up and let it filter through his hands. "Put your light on this," he told Christie, as he studied it.

"It's black," she said.

"Holy smoke!" he exclaimed, and then chuckled. "I mean, that's what it is—*charcoal!*"

"From the fire!" she said. "Then if there was an opening here—"

"The charcoal from the floors filled it," said Kevin, getting the same idea. "And when they cleared away

the debris, the earth got mixed in with it, and the whole thing was covered."

"If there *was* a passage, maybe nobody even discovered it," said Kevin, catching Christie's and Colum's excitement.

"Then only the ghost of the monk it is, as knows what's lying under here," said Colum, his eyes glittering. Without another word, he began to dig furiously.

At the opposite end of the trench, Kevin had gone down another foot when his spade rasped on stone. "If it's a boulder, your monk has double-crossed us," he said, "or worse, it could be a sub-flooring of stone. Maybe the whole tower goes down this deep—the walls, too, I mean—to keep their enemies from digging in from the outside."

"True," Colum admitted. "It was Padraic as said the walls go down to a great base of stone."

"But there, in the middle of the tower?" Christie questioned.

Colum shook his head. "No," he said, "if the monk pointed here, it is not a solid floor of stone."

"The monk!" Kevin exclaimed in disgust. "We don't know that there was a monk. We don't know what Chris saw. But we'll soon find out about this stone. Come on, help me dig around it—*if* we can!"

Together, the boys dug carefully, spading away the mixture of charcoal and earth in their search for the outer edges of the stone. As they uncovered it, they found that it was a flat slab of limestone, but it was wider than their trench. Cutting away the earth on each side, they struck stone again, but this was upraised above the one they had been uncovering.

"It's vertical," Kevin said. "We've reached a vertical wall on each side!"

"Then the flat one could be a step!" Christie exclaimed.

Without answering, the boys drove their spades into the soil on which they'd been standing. Less than a foot down, their spades rasped against stone once more. Scooping the soil out, they uncovered another flat slab of limestone.

"We've hit it!" Kevin shouted. "A walled stairway. I wonder how far down the steps go?" He jumped down on his spade. "If we dig side by side, we'll soon find out."

Together, they uncovered one step, and then another. Three feet of earth and charcoal had to be removed before they reached the wider slab that proved to be the landing.

As they uncovered it, their spades struck vertical stone again, but this was different. It, too, was a limestone slab, and as they knocked away the earth that clung to it, they realized that it was a sort of door, about four feet high and leaning at a slight slant away from the stairs. Further digging revealed that it was only two feet wide, supported on each side by rock walls.

"There it is," said Kevin, "the entrance to the secret passage!" His eyes, as Christie beamed the light down on them, were as bright as Colum's. "You led us to it, Chris, you and your monk, or whatever it was you saw," he added, not quite willing to accept the idea of a ghost.

The boys stared at the slab, pondering on whether they could move it. It was slightly askew, giving them a small opening at the lower corner, where they could grasp it. Too excited to wait, they threw down their spades, grasped the corner and tried to lift it. As they pulled, it slid toward them, and they leapt backwards just in time to save their toes from being crushed beneath its weight.

"Wow!" Kevin gasped. "That was close—but look what happened!"

In addition to sliding forward, the slab has slipped sideways, so that it was much more askew, with an upper corner wedged tightly against the stone wall of the stairs on one side, and a lower corner wedged solidly against the opposite wall.

"How lucky can we get?" Kevin said. "Nothing's going to budge that slab now, and we can crawl around it."

Colum was already on his knees, starting to snake his way through the opening.

"You'd better wait!" Kevin commanded sharply. He was remembering that Gypsies were habitual thieves, and since Christie had, unaccountably, been led to the secret passage, it might even be that they were now close to the treasure.

Colum, he knew, was thinking the same thing, and they had agreed that "finders" would be "keepers."

"I wouldn't want to follow a dead man in the dark," Kevin went on, counting on Colum's superstitious fear to stop him.

It worked. Colum backed out. He had left his flashlight on the ground six feet above them while he dug. Now Christie picked it up.

"Come on, Chris," Kevin said, and reaching up to

catch her as she jumped down to the first step, he took one flashlight from her.

Outside, the electrical storm was still raging. The great tower shuddered with the rolling of thunder, and the rain was beginning to drip down between the planks of the floor above them.

"If the ghost of your monk is going to lead us out of this firetrap, you'd better step aside and let Chris go first," Kevin told Colum. "She's the only one that can see him."

Grudgingly, Colum stepped aside, and Christie knelt at the opening.

"Go ahead, crawl in," Kevin urged her. "If lightning strikes this place, we'll be a lot safer underground. And I'll be right behind you, to protect you." He handed Colum the other flashlight. "It was your great-grandmother that gave me my orders, remember?" he said.

Christie crawled through the opening, beaming the flashlight ahead of her. "It's an underground tunnel with an arched ceiling and walls of stone," she said, moving farther in to allow Kevin and Colum to follow her.

It was a narrow passageway, and low, little more than the height of the four-foot slab door. Their twin beams lighted only the first few yards, leaving the rest of it in darkness.

"Do you see anything?" Kevin asked. "You know, I mean—" He couldn't bring himself to say "the ghost."

"There's too much light," Christie said.

"Then douse them."

Christie and Colum switched off the flashlights, and they found themselves staring blindly into utter blackness.

After a moment of silence, Colum whispered, "Are you seeing him now, Christie?"

"I—don't know," she replied hesitantly. "I think— maybe—but way down the passage. It's so far, I can't tell."

"Is it beckoning he is?"

"No," Christie said. "If it's the monk I'm seeing, he's just standing still."

"Waiting," said Colum, in a barely audible whisper.

The thought of a ghost waiting for them far down the dark passage sent cold shivers through the three of them, and though no one of them admitted it, their hearts were pounding uncomfortably.

"Then switch on the flashes, and let's go," Kevin said.

They walked slowly down the narrow tunnel, heads bent and shoulders hunched to avoid hitting the stone ceiling. The rock paving underfoot was some- what uneven, and they kept their lights focused on the area immediately ahead of them. But the image of a spectral figure had taken shape in their minds, and it lingered with them, haunting their every step.

"How about letting me lead?" Kevin asked. "The faster we go, the sooner we'll be out of here."

He changed places with Christie, and increased their pace, but walking faster did nothing to dispel the eerie atmosphere of the ancient tunnel or relieve their nervous apprehension.

Suddenly Kevin seemed to stumble, and at the

same instant, he doused his flashlight. Neither Christie nor Colum could see beyond him, for he managed to fill the narrow passage.

"There's a—a cave-in," he said. "You'll have to go around me. Flatten yourself against the left side of the tunnel, Chris, and edge along. I'll light your way."

He beamed the light closely upon the rock wall of the tunnel, so that it was confined to that area, and Christie moved past him sideways, but she had gone only a foot or so when she struck his arm and knocked the flash out of his hand. On the ground, the light revealed what he had been trying to hide from her: the skeleton of a man, lying in the mouldering remains of a monk's cassock.

Christie gasped with horror, but she didn't turn away.

Crowding forward, Colum let out a shocked whisper, "It's *him!*"

Kevin bent down and picked up his flash. "I didn't want you to see—" he began.

"He *wanted* me to see him," Christie said slowly. "He led me here. All these years he's been wanting someone to find him."

"I wonder why?" Kevin speculated.

Christie stared down at the skeleton, remembering old Sorcha's prophecy. She'd seen the ghost of the monk—she'd been led to the place where he'd died. There had to be a reason, and the reason had to be the treasure.

She knew that by now, Kevin and Colum were arriving at the same conclusion. But true to the Gypsy's prophecy, it was she who saw it. It lay, partially hidden, beneath the bones of the monk's chest. He must have clutched it to his breast, Christie thought, and fallen upon it in his last effort to protect it. It must be something very precious, for he had wanted it to be found.

Without fear, she knelt and drew from under his disintegrated cassock and the long-dry bones, a box about the size of a book. As Kevin beamed his flash onto it, she saw that it was covered with metal, and richly ornamented with the figures of people and animals in bold relief, and though it was blackened by time, Christie guessed that it must be fashioned of bronze or copper and silver and gold.

But before she could get a good look at it, Colum moved with sudden violence, pushing Kevin so that he staggered forward, almost falling onto the skeleton. As he tried to regain his balance, Colum snatched the box from Christie's hands and raced down the length of the dark tunnel, silhouetted by the beam of light that moved ahead of him.

12

Sorcha's Prophecy—the Danger

Kevin and Christie hurried in pursuit of Colum as swiftly as their hunched position in the low, cramped tunnel permitted. Kevin led the way, trying to share the pale beam of the one remaining flashlight with his sister. Shouting at Colum, he commanded him to stop, but the Gypsy ignored his calls, and suddenly his light and his silhouette disappeared from view.

Had he rounded a bend somewhere ahead of them? If so, Kevin thought, there should have been a receding reflection of the light along the wall. But if he'd fallen into a hole—or jumped?

Kevin slowed down, approaching more cautiously the place where Colum had vanished, and sent his flash beaming ahead to search for the cause.

"Kevin, I see him!" Christie whispered.

"Colum?" Kevin asked in surprise.

"No, the monk."

Again, she began to walk as though in a trance. This time she moved ahead of Kevin down the passage.

"What's he doing?" Kevin asked, humoring her.

"Beckoning to us," she said, in that same far-away voice.

She moved slowly along the passage, her eyes fixed on her vision of the monk, while Kevin followed, beaming his flash onto the uneven paving beneath their feet. Christie did not glance down, nor did she stumble.

They had gone several yards when she stopped suddenly and whispered, "Wait!"

"What now?" Kevin asked.

"He's pointing—"

"Where?"

"To our left," she said, her voice still strangely remote. "He wants us to turn to our left."

Kevin beamed the flash up onto the wall at their left.

"There's no opening," he said. "We can't go through the stone."

"We're not quite there yet," she said. "I think he wants us to come to where he is."

"Where's that?" said Kevin, sending the light ahead of her down the passage.

"I can't see him now," she answered. "He disappeared when you turned the light onto him."

But Kevin saw why Colum, too, had vanished. A few feet ahead of them the stone-walled tunnel ended abruptly in a cavern created not by the monks but by nature itself.

Somehow, those centuries ago, the monks had discovered the stream-deserted passage of an underground river and used it as their secret trail to
freedom and safety. They had built their tunnel to
an opening in the wall of the cave—or broken
through it themselves—and now Kevin and Christie
saw why Colum had disappeared so suddenly. The
floor of the cave was some six or seven feet below the
tunnel, and in his frantic haste to escape, he must
have come upon it too quickly to do anything but
jump. Whether he had suffered any injury or not, he
had managed to go on, for there was no sign of him
or of the treasure. The cave was empty.

Kevin took the descent more wisely, first kneeling,
then swinging down, his hands gripping the stones
of the tunnel floor until he let go to make the final
short drop. Christie followed, swinging down until
her feet rested firmly on her brother's shoulders, and
from there he helped her to descend gently to the
ground.

The cave was small and it tapered up to a pointed
arch which was split at the top by a great crack that
stretched beyond sight into the dark rock of the roof.
The floor was of dry, hard mud, but Colum's sprawl-
ing fall on hands and knees had left its mark, as had
his running footprints. He had turned to the left, just
as Christie's monk had directed them to do—*if* she
had seen his ghost. Kevin noted that there was a sort
of luminescence in the arch of the cave. Perhaps that
was what she had seen.

Kevin and Christie followed the footprints down
a long gallery that maintained the high, pointed arch
of the cave. The comfort of walking upright after the

low tunnel was a relief, but the passage narrowed and curved as it sloped down at a 30° angle, and they were still unable to catch even a glimpse of the thieving Gypsy.

Racing down the dry streamway, they were brought to an unexpected halt by a side passage that branched off to the right. The mud floor had grown increasingly hard, but careful study revealed that the footprints turned off, instead of following the main gallery straight ahead. Perhaps Colum had taken the side passage to elude them, without realizing that he was leaving a faint but discernible trail behind him. Whatever his reason, there were no other prints to follow, and they took the side passage.

It, too, sloped downwards and they became aware of fine stalactite pendants hanging from the roof. At any other time, they would have stopped to admire them, but in the urgency of their chase they couldn't afford to pause. The passage steepened, forcing them to step with care lest they skid down into the unknown darkness beyond the beam of their flashlight.

The hard mud under their feet became softer, and Kevin stopped abruptly, realizing that if Colum had preceded them, there should be footprints. There were none.

He sent the light down in a long beam ahead of them, and though distance weakened it, he caught the shimmer of water.

"Wait here," he told Christie.

"In the dark?" she protested.

"For just a second," he said. "I've got to make sure."

"Of what?"

But Kevin had already moved ahead, searching the soft mud from wall to wall. No one could have gotten through without leaving prints. The passage ended suddenly in a deep pit filled with water, and Kevin was grateful that he and Christie hadn't skidded down into it. But obviously Colum hadn't either, for there was no imprint of footstep or sliding body.

He climbed back up to Christie. "The passage dead-ends in a deep pool and Colum hasn't been down there," he said. "Either he tricked us, or he was a long way ahead, and by now he's really had a chance to make time. We'll never catch him unless he dead-ends in some long passage."

"The whole thing could dead-end in a river like the one you almost drowned in," said Christie, starting to climb up.

"Don't forget the ten monks that got out," Kevin said.

"That was a long time ago," Christie reminded him. "The river could have changed its course."

"Don't worry, there'll be a way out," said Kevin reassuringly, but he knew she was right.

They climbed back up to the main gallery and raced down its hard mud slope, not noticing the graceful scalloping on the walls made by the flow of that long-ago river; not even pausing to search for Colum's footprints, for they knew now that this was the only way he could have gone.

At length, they emerged into a large cavern, covered with a huge pile of boulders which had, presumably, fallen from the roof. Kevin scanned it with roughly triangular in shape, its nearly level floor his flash. The walls were covered with beautiful dripstone formations deposited through the centuries by the dripping of water into the cave, and from what remained of the ceiling, the dripstone hung in folds like curtains, and there were single stalactites tapering down like icicles.

Christie would have liked to let her eyes linger on the remarkable shapes and designs, but Kevin had his mind on only one thing: a passage that would lead them through and beyond the cavern. There was nothing visible on the near side of the boulders. That meant they would have to climb over them.

The great mass of rock was ten feet high at its lowest point, and the ascent was rough and slow, with Kevin having to light each boulder for Christie so that she could see the narrow but treacherous crevices between them. Halfway up the pile, he switched off his flash. From somewhere ahead of him, on the down side of the mass, he thought he had glimpsed a faint glimmer of light.

Left suddenly in darkness, Christie started to speak, but he hushed her with a whisper, and together they saw the faint reflection moving down the far wall of the cave. It had to be Colum's flashlight!

"Colum!" Kevin shouted. "We know you're there, and you're not going to get away. You're slowing up already and we know why!"

He was remembering Colum's leap down from the tunnel to the first cave and gambling on the fact that he might have hurt or sprained a knee or ankle.

The light had been switched off, and they were all in total darkness.

"Colum," Kevin went on persuasively, "you can't

make it. We'll be up with you in a minute, so why not stop now? The treasure belongs to Chris. Your own great-grandmother said so."

"She only said I'd *find* it," Christie whispered. "She didn't say I'd keep it."

"Sh!" They listened and heard a faint sound of something scraping softly over rock. "He's trying to go on down in the dark," Kevin said, and switched on his own flash. "We've got to keep going." He kept his light beamed on the small area of their own climb, so as not to light the way for the Gypsy boy.

"You can't go against your own great-grand-mother," Kevin shouted again. "Stop now, Colum, and we'll call it quits and find our way out of here together."

There was no answer, but Colum's light was on again, and they knew he was scrambling down the pile as swiftly as he could go. They were still several feet from the top, and he was safely out of sight.

"Please, Colum," Christie called desperately, "it isn't for me I want the treasure. It's for the monk and for Ireland."

Colum did not respond, and the reflection of his light was almost lost to them.

"Please, Colum, I beg you, don't sell it!" Christie pleaded. "It's a precious antiquity, and it should go to the museum in Dublin."

Kevin had climbed in a rush to the top, and now he turned back to light Christie's way.

"He's gone," he said disgustedly, "and if we don't catch him, the museum will never get the treasure. He'll unload it to the first buyer, and probably for a fraction of its worth."

"Maybe he won't," said Christie, climbing. "Maybe he'll sell it to the museum. Even if they have to buy it, it'll be better than losing it entirely."

"He'd never dare take it to them. They'd be sure he'd stolen it."

They made the slow, difficult descent down the boulder mass, and at the bottom discovered a tunnel. This must have been Colum's escape route, for if there was any other passage out of the cavern, they couldn't see it.

It was a low tunnel and they had to crawl, but fortunately it was short, and they were soon climbing down stalagmite "steps" formed by a residual drip from the roof of the gallery they were entering. For a hundred feet and more they were able to run upright in a long curve, and then to their intense disappointment, it closed down to an impassible stalagmited fissure. But this time it seemed that they would not have to return. Just short of the fissure, another small tunnel ascended out of the gallery, and they crawled up it gratefully, only to find themselves coming out of a hole between boulders. They were in the huge cavern they had just left, facing again the great pile of rocks. The gallery and the ascending tunnel had taken them back in an almost perfect circle to the place where they had started.

Had Colum suffered the same fate! they wondered. If so, he must be somewhere in the cave with them now—unless he had found another exit. He would not go back to the tower and face the danger of fire.

Kevin probed among the rocks along the wall of the cave and to his amazement, found a hole beneath a boulder. It was no more than twenty inches high and even less wide, but Colum had gone through it, for there was a piece of cloth from his pants caught on a jagged edge of stone.

While Christie stood by, he lay down and squeezed into it. He could not see Colum, but he found a low passage and knew Colum had taken it.

He hated to bring Christie into such a place, but he couldn't explore it without a light, and he couldn't leave her behind in the dark. Besides, Colum and the stolen treasure were only a part of the problem. Even more important, they had to find a way out.

With Christie following close on his heels, he worked his way down the sloping hole in a flat-out crawl, edging forward on elbows and hips and pushing with his feet until the ceiling raised and the passage widened, but it was still too low for walking, and there was an uncomfortable 60° dip to the left.

The floor was covered with small stalagmite knobs, which made their continued crawl painful, and here and there, thick stalagmite columns joined the low roof to the floor, so that they had to wriggle around and between them.

Near the end of the long, tortuous passage they sighted a whole forest of straw stalactites. These, too, joined roof to floor and even with their bodies turned sideways, the pipestem formations threatened to block their way, but when they reached them, they discovered that they were thin-walled tubes of translucent calcite, and Colum had already broken through, leaving the fractured stalactites to mark his trail. Kevin wondered how far ahead he was, and whether there was really any chance that they could catch up with him.

The passage ended in a broad cave and they were grateful that its dome gave them standing room, for their muscles were cramped and aching. At the upper end of the chamber, a flowstone cascade seemed to pour from the wall onto the floor like a frozen river, and there were several small crawl holes, any one of which Colum might have taken, but Kevin gave his first attention to a fissure at the lower end. Beaming his light down through the crack, he saw another cavity directly beneath them. Its floor was covered with a heavy layer of soft mud in which there were soggy and unmistakably fresh footprints.

"Chris, he jumped down there," Kevin whispered excitedly, "and not too long ago, or that wet mud would have closed over his prints. We've got to get down there fast."

"Into that awful mud?" Christie protested. "We

don't know how deep it is, and there must be water nearby—maybe a river."

"I could go alone and faster," said Kevin, "but you don't want to stay here in the dark, do you?"

"I do not!" Christie whispered, a cold shiver running up her spine. "In this crazy maze of tunnels, you might never find me again."

"Then come on. We'll go down the same way we went down from the monks' tunnel into that first cave."

The rift in the floor was thickly coated with dripstone flow and barely wide enough to permit their passage, but Kevin swung down first, his landing softened by the mud, and then eased Christie down after him.

She had been right: the mud was unexpectedly deep, and he felt himself sinking into it as he caught and supported her weight. Urging her to crawl over it quickly, he struggled out of its sucking grip and followed, for she had been right about the river, too, and they were crossing a mud bank to reach it. Flowing silently, it curved between cave-wall and bank, and to their relief it proved to be no more than a foot deep, with a fairly smooth stone bed beneath it.

The roof over their heads rose gradually from four to a good fifteen feet, and when they'd washed off what mud they could, they began to walk downstream in the cold water. Colum, too, had crossed the bank to walk in the river, leaving no clues behind him.

They moved cautiously on the slippery stone between walls scalloped and curtained and hung with fascinating formations, but their thoughts were on

the Gypsy, and Kevin beamed the flash from right to
left, scanning every foot for crawl-holes or tunnels
that might have served as escape passages or hiding
places. He found none.

A second stream entered from a low rift at one
side, and there was no longer any mud bank. The
river filled the gallery from wall to wall, not deepening but flowing more swiftly downslope. Kevin and
Christie had no choice but to follow it, the danger
growing as the water swirled and sped around them,
the pull of it strengthening as the slope steepened.

Gradually they became aware of a sound louder
than the rush of the stream. Somewhere ahead, there
was the roar of water *falling*.

They slowed their pace, clinging to the textured
walls, while Kevin searched the shadowed gallery as
far ahead as the small beam of his flash would reach.
He spotted a third stream rushing down from a hole
in the wall, some two feet above the river. The roar
increased as they approached it, but the sound was
greater than that of a two-foot fall, and as they
inched nervously around a curve in the passage, they
saw the real cause: some twenty feet ahead of them,
the bed of the river split apart, leaving a large rift in
the middle. The waters rushed into it, plunging down
to the darkness below.

Beyond the opening of the rift, the stone floor of
the passage continued on each side, like two wide
shelves hanging in space. Kevin and Christie walked
cautiously out onto the shelf at the left of the fissure.
The beam of the flash showed them that the waters
fell into a dark river or lake some fifteen feet below.
They followed the shelf as it tapered out to a sudden

ending, while the rift widened, and saw that beyond
them stretched an enormous cave, filled wall to wall
with a great body of black water.

Christie stared at it, appalled. "This is the end,"
she murmured, hardly able to accept the terrifying
finality of it. "There's no place to go!"

"Colum!" said Kevin, suddenly remembering the
Gypsy boy. "He went somewhere—and not into that
lake!"

"But where?" Christie asked. "We didn't meet
him, and there wasn't a single crawl hole or tunnel
along the river."

Kevin turned abruptly and looked behind him at
the wall that rose up from the shelf. In their preoccu-
pation with the waterfall and the lake, they hadn't
thought to look for a passage beyond the point where
the river fell into the rift.

"Look there!" he whispered, beaming his flash onto
a low opening in the wall. He crept back to it, and
peering inside, saw that it was a steep, water-scal-
loped passage that ascended like a slanting chimney
for about twelve feet. Beyond that, it curved out of
sight, but he was sure Colum had gone up there.

"Chris," he whispered, "the climb is steep and if it
comes to a dead-end, I can catch him. If he's not
there, it may mean we've found a way out. Wait here
for me!"

"In the dark?" Christie cried in shock.

"For just a minute. I can't take time to get us
both up. It could mean I'd lose him."

"I don't care!"

"Please, Chris, just stay where you are and don't
move. I'll be right back."

Kevin had crawled through the opening and was already climbing up the steep chimney-passage before Christie could stop him. She stood on the narrow shelf, the rift wide and black in front of her, while the faint illumination of Kevin's flashlight faded as he ascended until she was left in total darkness, hearing only the roar of the waters.

Time seemed to stretch out interminably, and her body tightened with the tension of waiting, while the horror of being alone in the vast blackness grew inside her until her heart hammered in her chest and she felt as if she were suffocating.

Out of the darkness, she thought she heard Kevin's voice. The sound was distant and muffled by the roar of the waterfall. She moved cautiously out toward the end of the ledge to get away from the plunging waters, and heard him again. He was shouting her name and something more, but she couldn't hear the words.

Suddenly a light was beamed down onto the stone shelf from a fissure in the wall that she hadn't seen before. There was a scuffing sound behind her, and Colum hurtled down and burst out of the opening, striking her full force as he ran. The blow knocked her off the ledge, and she screamed in terror as she fell toward the black waters.

13
The Cumdach

Descending the passage just seconds behind Colum, Kevin heard Christie's scream, but when he rushed out of the fissure she had disappeared.

Colum had been stopped in his tracks by her shriek of terror, and stood stunned, beaming his light down onto the black lake.

"What happened?" Kevin yelled. "Where's Chris?

Colum stared at him, speechless with shock, and at that moment Christie rose, struggling, to the surface. Instantly, Kevin laid his flashlight on the stone shelf and jumped. The water was deep, and his body went far down into the cold darkness before he could fight his way up and swim to his sister. She was thrashing violently, going under and rising again, for the sudden horror of her backward fall had sent her into temporary shock. When Kevin reached her, she

struggled against him, instinctively fighting for her
life, without knowing what she was doing. He
gripped her strongly in his arms, talking to her
soothingly while he treaded water, until at length
she relaxed, reoriented by his words and his presence.
When he looked up to the shelf, Colum had disappeared.

The fissure rose above them, a sheer stone precipice
impossible to climb. Kevin's flash lay where he had
left it, sending its little beam out into the black
immensity of the cavern. There was no other light.

Christie's strength was spent, and supporting her, Kevin swam out toward the middle of the lake, away from the turbulence of the falls. There, he stopped, treading water while they studied the scene. The roof of the cave was a high arch lost in shadows, and though the walls showed only dimly, it was obvious that they curved down to a sudden drop, as sheer as that of the fissure. There could be no hope of climbing any of them.

"We'll never get out," said Christie, her voice breaking.

"Oh, yes, we will!" Kevin declared positively, though in his heart he was as doubtful as she.

"How?" she asked. "We're trapped in the middle of a huge lake far underground, and even that little light won't last indefinitely. The batteries will give out."

Kevin had thought of that already. "I've got to find a way out of here before they do." He scanned the opposite shore of the lake. It, too, was lost in shadows, but it seemed to him that there was something hopeful about its shape.

"Look, Chris," he said. "I think there's something different on that side, a ledge, maybe. Just relax and I'll take you over."

"I can swim now," she said.

They swam together toward the far shore, and it was indeed different. The abrupt drop of the wall changed, near its base, to a gentle slope, so that it almost had the look of a small beach. It was hard rock and its slope continued underwater, but they climbed onto it, grateful for a chance to rest on something solid.

"Colum ran away, didn't he?" Christie asked, after a moment.

"Yeah."

"His hitting me was an accident."

"I figured that."

"Do you think he'll do anything to help us?"

"I'm not sure he could if he wanted to," Kevin said. "He's better off than we are, but that doesn't mean he'll find a way out—or even a way back to the tower. And besides, he's got the treasure."

"I know." She paused, wondering if he would

abandon them for the price of it. "Did that last tunnel lead up to a deadend?" she asked finally.

"I didn't have time to find out. It was another cave full of boulders. I happened to corner Colum, and he scooted down the first hole he saw."

"And collided with me!"

"Rotten luck!" said Kevin bitterly. "If I hadn't gone up after him—"

"You were looking for a way out."

"Yeah, and there might have been one somewhere among those boulders."

"Which way did Colum go?"

"I don't know. He took off after I jumped into the water."

Kevin pulled off his wet sweater and pants and his soaked loafers. "And I'd better get back in before that light dims," he said, sliding down the stone slope.

"What are you going to do?" Christie asked anxiously.

"Swim around the rim of this lake and see if I can find a way out."

His sister shivered with cold and apprehension. "Be careful!" she pleaded urgently.

"You, too. Don't fall asleep and slip off that rock."

He pushed off before she could answer, and began his swim around the precipitous walls of the cavern. They were coved like palisades bordering the sea, and in examining every sheer foot, he had to stroke into and around every curve, so that the circumference of the cave was doubled.

Christie tried to follow with her eyes, but the little beam from the flashlight was dim and far away, and he was soon swallowed up in the darkness of the coves. She felt lost and alone in a nightmare world, and her thoughts went back to the locket with its sacred ashes. Would she and Kevin be here now, she wondered, if Ben hadn't stolen it and dropped it into the river?

The old Gypsy, and Mrs. O'Flaherty, too, had been sure of its power to protect. She remembered the white mare with her foal at Aughnanure castle. Wild as she had later proven to be, the mare had looked at her with gentleness while she was wearing it. It was after she had dropped it and Ben had snatched it away, that their troubles had begun. Without the locket, would they ever escape from this frightening underground trap? If only she had it in her hands now, Christie thought, it would give her such hope. Unconsciously, she put her hand to her chest, pressing the place where it had lain.

Kevin stopped, chilled and aching after a long strenuous pull, and clung to the water-scarred wall, breathing heavily as he rested. He had gone more than a third of the distance around the lake, reaching up to feel the wall with his hands where it was darkest, and letting his feet explore the underwater contours of the rock. He had found nothing to give him hope. The walls rose sharply to the arched roof above, or dipped to the depths below, completely solid in both directions, without even a hint of a hole or fissure.

He was nearly opposite Christie now, but he couldn't see her.

"Chris!" he shouted, his voice echoing across the

cavern. "You there?"

"Here!" she shouted back, her answer blurred by the echo, and the sound of the waterfall. "Find anything?"

"Not yet," he shouted, and after the echo had died, he added reassuringly, "but I will, soon!"

He began to swim again, passing the rift and the waterfall. The flashlight on the shelf was beamed away from him, and the area he was exploring was in almost total darkness. Touching the walls above and below water, his heart leapt suddenly with hope as he reached out into space—an open space just below the surface.

He paused to rest a moment, then sucked in a deep breath and went under, feeling his way carefully. It could be just a cavity in the rock, he realized, a cavity leading nowhere. He stroked on, beginning to feel a pain in his chest. In only seconds more, he'd have to turn back. Suddenly he became aware of a dim light somewhere ahead of him. Swimming desperately toward it, he shot up, his lungs bursting. Filling them with air, he saw that he was in a small cave with a "skylight" at the top. It was far beyond his reach, but it was an opening onto the world of the living. In the middle of the cavity, a pile of boulders jutted up above the water-line. In falling from the roof, they had opened the hole to the sky.

Jubilantly, he sucked in air again and went back through the black rift to get Christie before she might be lost to him in darkness.

When he had pulled her safely through the underwater passage, they climbed up onto the boulders and looked at the hole above them.

"It's like coming alive after being buried in a tomb!" Christie cried joyfully.

"We're a long way from being out," Kevin warned.

"About thirty feet," Christie cut in.

"Without a ladder or a rope it might as well be three hundred," said Kevin. "We can't make it on our own."

They studied the opening. It was generally round, like the top of a deep well, and it must be entirely cut off from view on the ground above, they thought, for it was surrounded by thick shrubs and hung with trailing vines, none of them long enough or strong enough to be of any use.

"The storm is over," Christie said, noting that the sky was no longer black, and white clouds were moving across the small open space, showing cracks of brilliant blue between them.

"We can yell for help," she said. "Maybe someone will hear us."

"Who?" asked Kevin. "There was nothing around that tower but ruined farmhouses and the ruined monastery."

"And a healing well that people come to," said Christie, remembering, "and a road."

"We'll yell our heads off," said Kevin, "but it may be a long wait." He began to shout "Help, help!" and Christie joined him. They yelled until their throats gave out and they had to rest, but there was no answer.

They heard a distant rumbling. It couldn't be thunder, for the sky was clearing, growing bluer every moment as the clouds passed.

"It's a car or a cart passing over," said Kevin, with sudden conviction. "We *are* near a road."

He began to shout again, and Christie screamed for help with him, but the rumbling sound receded until it had faded entirely. The vehicle, whatever it was, had passed without hearing them, the noise of its own wheels or motor probably drowning out their voices.

They rested awhile, listening, but there was no recurrence of the rumble.

"It's probably a little old side road that hardly anyone uses," said Kevin.

Christie began to yell again, and he added his shouts to hers. They paused, and heard the cawing of a crow.

"Ben!" Christie cried. "It could be Ben!"

They shouted again, wildly, calling his name. The cawing came closer, and soon they saw the black outline of a crow against the blue sky.

"Ben! Ben, it's us!" they shrieked in joy and hope.

The crow dipped lower, cawing as he circled above the shrubs. They yelled, and his caws seemed to grow louder and more excited as he glided and dipped just above the opening.

A human voice was approaching, and the words were Gaelic. The shrubs parted and Colum peered down the pit.

"Holy Mother!" he whispered. "Is it really you I'm seeing?"

What better rescuer could they have hoped for than a friend who had found his own way out of the cave, and then, with the aid of a rope and a strong Connemara pony, pulled them to safety?

No one had spoken of the treasure, but as they climbed into the two-wheeled cart, Colum said, "It's in the straw you'll find the cumdach."

"Find what?" asked Kevin in surprise.

"Christie's treasure. It was out of my head I was, snatching it away from you, but at the sight of it a sort of madness came over me, and I could think of nothing but the gold it would bring. It was a madness kept me running, and then the shame, for I couldn't turn back to face you after the stealing of it. And when I bumped into you, Christie, and saw you fall, my wits went out of me altogether, and my words with them. But now I have them back, and you have your cumdach, for it's the truth I was telling you: Gypsies steal no big things. And a cumdach is a big thing, indeed—a treasure worth more gold than I could use if I traveled all the roads of the world put together." He grinned impishly. "Had it been a small thing, I'd have stolen it, surely."

"You would not," said Christie softly, her eyes brimming with tears. "You came back to find us."

"That I did, and missed you entirely I might have, but for Ben. It was he was the real rescuer."

Perched on Colum's head, Ben made a self-satisfied comment.

Christie lifted the straw and saw the precious box carefully cushioned in a safe corner.

"It's Padraic can tell you what it is," said Colum, clucking to his horse.

When they reached the O'Flaherty farm and all of them had gathered together to stare in wonder at the treasure, Padraic did explain what it was. Colum had been right: it was called a "cumdach," which was a book box, or shrine, made to protect an object believed to have belonged to a saint, or a manuscript relating to his history. Every cumdach, because of the valued relic inside of it, had had a keeper who was responsible for its safety, and the dead monk must have been the custodian of the cumdach of Kilvarra.

The box itself was about eight inches high by six wide, and some two inches thick, made of wood covered with metal sheets. Though its surface was now dull and dark, Padraic assured them that both the sheets themselves and the figures that stood out in bold relief against the patterned metal were made of bronze covered with silver and gold. They seemed to be angels and perhaps warriors, surrounded by animals, all shaped to fit into a beautiful design, and the box, he thought, must have been made as far back as the eleventh century.

When Christie opened it, she found inside the relic it had been made to protect: a manuscript written by hand on parchment, and decorated with ornamental capitals. It might be a fragment of a saint's gospel, Padraic thought, and she didn't touch it for fear of damaging something so very old and sacred.

"Sorcha was right," Padraic said, as Christie gently closed the box. "It is indeed a priceless treasure, and now that you have found it, what is it you're planning to be doing with it, Christie lass?"

"I'm going to give it to the National Museum at Dublin with the name of three donors," she said, "myself and Kevin and Colum O'Halloran."

And that night at the Gypsy camp there was a great sound of music, with violin and accordion accompanying the singing and dancing of the O'Hallorans and the O'Flahertys and the American MacAlistaires, all celebrating together the finding of the treasure of the monastery of Kilvarra.

ELIZABETH BALDWIN HAZELTON
has had many years of
experience in writing for
radio and television. Among
other outstanding scripts,
she has done a score of
television screenplays for the
series *Death Valley Days.*
Miss Hazelton has also been a
professional actress and for
twelve years taught radio and
television writing in Los
Angeles. She now lives and
works in South Laguna,
California, in a house
overlooking the Pacific Ocean.
Her other books for young
people are *Tides of Danger*
(1967), *The Day the Fish
Went Wild* (1969), *Sammy,
the Crow Who Remembered*
(1969), *The Jade Eagle*
(1970), and *The Haunted
Cove* (1971).